Up ❧

All

Night

Also by Delilah Dawson

Something Naughty

Truth or Dare

Mr. Satisfaction

Delilah Dawson

Up & All Night

St. Martin's Griffin
New York

This is a work of fiction. All of the characters, organizations, and events portrayed in this novel are either products of the author's imagination or are used fictitiously.

www.stmartins.com

Design by Kathryn Parise

ISBN-13: 978-0-312-36936-1
ISBN-10: 0-312-36936-0

First Edition: June 2008

10 9 8 7 6 5 4 3 2 1

To my sisters and friends
who have been with me through essential cappuccinos,
precarious semicolons, and heavenly pedicures.
Thank you!

Up All Night

Prologue ❧

I t's all about the sex, ladies. And Orchid Soul is it!"

As far as presentations went, Eileen's statements were brief and to the point. Natasha Madison and her friends joined the smatter of claps when they realized that was the extent of the presentation.

Across the dinner table from Natasha, Eileen flashed her troublemaker grin. "So, are you in?"

"Hell, yeah!" Vanessa piped in, then quickly elbowed Natasha, who nodded and said, "Sure!"

She, in turn, elbowed Rusty, who found all eyes on her. "I don't know."

Natasha rolled her eyes. "Girl, it's not even real. We're just testing. What's not to know?"

"It's bad enough to fake it during sex, but to sign up for a fake fantasy sex club seems pretty damned sad, ladies," Rusty grumbled.

"Think of it as safe sex," Natasha teased.

"I don't want any sex at all," Rusty responded.

Vanessa shifted in her chair and raised an eyebrow at her friend. "Hey, I think you need to adopt Natasha's Diamond Life goals."

Natasha groaned, but her friends ignored her. She'd come up with the four C's after her ex-boyfriend had cheated on her—the loser.

"What were the four C's, Natasha? Clarity and . . . um . . ."

"Control," Rusty helped out.

"Conviction? Or is that Contraception?" Vanessa asked, already chuckling. "Because that definitely ought to be on the list."

"You're such a goofball," Natasha laughed.

"Wait, we're missing the last one. What is it?"

All eyes went to Natasha.

"Courage," she said, then looked at Rusty. "Courage, my sister."

Rusty put her hands out in defeat. "Okay, okay, I'm in."

As the dinner went on, thoughts of the four C's kept running through Natasha's mind. Following them was turning out to be harder than she'd expected.

In the last few months, she'd found herself taking them on, one by one.

Clarity had happened when she'd come home early to find her fiancé and her neighbor writhing in the same bed. Hell, how had she been so blind? Somehow, she'd managed to turn her fury into a hard chill that kept her from going into a wild rage that would've killed them both. As the saying went, hindsight was always crystal clear. All the little signs had been there, if she'd only looked.

Control. She wasn't going to ever get played like that again.

Courage. It was really one step up from caution, but truly, once bitten, twice shy.

Conviction. This was the toughest part. It was easy to think of clarity, control, and courage in logical terms, but, God, it was so much harder to get the true conviction to believe it of herself.

Diamonds were one of the toughest things on earth, so calling her philosophy Diamond Life seemed appropriate.

Besides, Orchid Soul was the perfect place to start practicing.

Eileen's debut party—or rather, as Eileen called it, *debug* party—was turning out to be a hit.

Not, however, for Natasha. The low-level energy had her craving cigarettes again. There was an unmistakable sense of desperation in the air. Too much testosterone. Too many women preening, eyeballing the men like starving barracudas. No different from the bar scenes she'd been to lately. Sure, Eugene had been a failure, but a girl had needs. She had to get back on the horse, so to speak . . . work on the whole courage thing.

She took a deep breath and tried to shake off the nerves as she wandered around the crowded party, looking for her best friends. When she didn't spot them, she headed for the patio doors.

Natasha slid her hand into her purse, immediately searching for a pack of gum, her mind wandering to her ex-fiancé. She'd dumped him along with her old, nasty habit of smoking, but every now and then, the cravings for both were vicious. It was surprising how much stronger the cravings for sex were getting.

The February night was warm and sticky in comparison with the air-conditioned ballroom, and once the door was closed, the R & B thump of music and conversation was muted significantly. As Murphy's Law would have it, there was an ashtray next to the door, brimming with cigarette butts. Even that old, stale scent had her groaning. Sure, they were rank and old, but cravings made her want to dig her nose into them like a bouquet of flowers.

Healthy choices. She was determined to make healthy, smart choices and stay in *control*! Who knew baby steps could be so hard?

Resigned to her goal, she rolled up her gum lengthwise, put it momentarily on her lips like she used to do with her lit cigarettes, then reluctantly and slowly, she took bites until it was completely in her mouth.

"That work?"

Natasha almost screamed at the gruff, male voice that caressed out of the surrounding darkness. She managed not to choke on the gum and glared at the moving shadow not far to her right.

As if in apology, a tall man stepped out into the dim light.

He was built like a corn-fed linebacker, his head full of braids that fell to his shoulders, making him look somewhat intimidating. The only movement appeared to be a plastic stir straw clamped tightly between his white teeth.

"It works," she replied, glad that her voice remained cool, revealing none of her sudden nerves.

He stepped closer, exposing more of his angular face to the light: his firm lips; his dark, narrowed eyes against skin as rich as freshly roasted coffee beans. Everything from his jeans, shirt, and boots showed signs of rough wear. As if he'd been riding his motorcycle in a mad dash to make it to the party on time.

But there was a surliness about him that hinted of nicotine withdrawal.

It was silly, really, for her heart to be doubling up on palpitations, not to mention the ghostly little flutter in her gut. *Sweet man candy!*

She tried not to show her reaction to him but realized she'd stopped chewing her gum.

The man tipped his head a bit and his braids followed the motion, fascinating her. She'd never dated anyone with braids or brawny muscles before. But she'd strongly consider him for one-night-stand material.

Nonetheless, as far as first impressions went, this guy was losing points. No witty conversation. Just, "That work?" What kind of a line was that? On the other hand, why worry about his IQ when he had a body like that?

She worked her way back up to his face and watched as the plastic straw moved to the other side of his mouth, but the faint smile that graced his lips had a sarcastic slant that made her realize she'd been staring way too long.

He cleared his throat and spoke around the mangled straw. "See anything you like?"

She blinked, felt her face redden, and wished she could blow a disdainful puff of smoke in his direction. "The jacket's not bad."

The smirk on his face turned into a slow grin.

"And maybe the boots, too."

He looked down at his jacket. "Didn't think it was your type of thing."

"It's not." She snapped her gum, smiling cheekily. "But looking ain't the same as shopping."

"Are we still talking about the clothes or the man?" he asked.

"There's an old saying that the clothes make the man," she noted.

There was amusement and challenge in his eyes when he chuckled. "See, that's where you're wrong."

"Really? So I shouldn't read much into the whole motorcycles-leather-and-chains look, huh?"

He shifted, and the play of light made it seem as if he was holding the night at bay. "Depends on what you are referring to . . . sex or transportation. I happen to like motorcycles for transportation, but when it comes to sex, velvet ropes and secluded stairwells or dungeons are more of my thing—"

"Okay!" She put her hands out as if she could hold back his words. "I get your point. We are not each other's types. I get it."

"I didn't say that." He grinned with smooth charm that lit up his features. "It's a personal policy of mine not to be discriminating or judgmental."

She flushed again, but before she could open her mouth to retaliate, he was already chuckling again. "Boy, you sure rile up easy."

Rather than give him the satisfaction of knowing how much his comment had hit its mark, she bit her lip. God, she craved a cigarette—longed to crush it dramatically into the ashtray, say something cutting, and make a grand exit.

A small pause followed, in which they eyed each other.

"Sorry," he said, leveling his disarming charm at her again. "I get grouchy when I need a smoke. Didn't mean to get your hackles up. Forgive me?"

She narrowed her gaze at him. "Let me think about it."

He suddenly moved a step closer, as quietly as smoke shifted by wind. She didn't have time to react before he reached out to gently touch the string of pearls at her neck. The warm contact stirred the strand and caused her nipples to pucker instantly. "Nice. Family heirloom?"

The change of subject had her thoughts scrambling.

The necklace was a graduation gift from her mother a few years back. One of many such presents, actually. It went well with most of her work attire at the law firm, so she felt obliged to wear them.

"You could say that." She hoped he hadn't noticed the sudden breathlessness in her reply.

"It's very . . . professional. You wear them well." There was a natural gravelly, husky tone to his voice that brought to mind seductive bedroom whispers and slow, skin-licking underwear removal. The light scent of his cologne teased her, making her want to lean closer.

What was he trying to prove?

She almost asked the question but instead pressed her lips together to hold it back. His gaze followed the movement, and for one long, insane second, she actually thought he was going to kiss her. She held her breath and her lips tingled, awaiting the contact.

There was the slightest shift in his breathing, and when his studious, probing gaze locked with hers, she knew without a doubt that it would not be a brief, stolen kiss. The glance couldn't have been more than a second, but it stretched out like an eternity.

The high pitch of her phone suddenly shrilled into the

moment and the spell was shattered, unlocking the breath Natasha had been holding.

"Excuse me," she said, turning away from him to answer her phone. Her mouth was dry when she said, "Hello?"

Her friend Rusty's voice boomed in her ear. "Hey, girl, where you at? Vanessa and I grabbed a corner booth not far from the bar, so when you come in, look for us."

Natasha didn't bother explaining that she was already at the party, hanging out on the patio with a stranger. Instead she agreed to meet them in a short while.

Just before she hung up, the man gave her a polite nod, his expression calm, as if nothing had happened. Then he quietly disappeared into the crowd indoors.

One ✿

Let the games begin," Natasha muttered as she turned off her computer, then reclined back in her chair. No doubt Eileen was a brilliant scientist, but the idea that there was math that could analyze her profile and determine who would be her partner—forever, no less—was laughable.

Thank God it was all anonymous and untraceable. Eileen had promised that much.

She kicked off her low-heeled sling backs and reached for

the three hairpins that held her coiffure firmly in place. Her straightened hair tumbled past her shoulders, and she sighed with relief as the tension on her scalp eased.

Standing, she did a few simple yoga stretches to ease the kinks in her back, then released a cleansing breath just as her PDA lit up and vibrated, indicating a text message.

Frowning, she picked it up from the table and read.

FROM: OrchidSoul.com

MESSAGE: A potential partner has been identified for you, and a compatibility report has been created for your review. If you approve of the report, an informal meeting will be scheduled. Please log on to proceed to the next phase.

"Already?" Hadn't it said it would take hours to do its thing? Obviously the system was flawed. Was her personality lacking such complexity that it had come up with a partner for her in less than ten minutes? Hell, it had taken much, much longer to fill out the intrusive questionnaire!

That definitely had to be a bug.

With a sigh, Natasha logged in successfully to the Web site and was presented with a "Male Candidate One" report.

Age: Within five year bracket (as specified)

Commonalities

Sports: None

Most free time: Varies

Extracurricular Activities: Poetry jams

Most unifying indicators:

7 keywords in both profiles indicate adventurous tendencies.

Natasha had to chuckle before moving on. That was it? Seven words, and bam, that meant she was adventurous?

Day one, and the system had already made her a skeptic.

> Statistically, the probability factor is 83.7% that this match is compatible.
>
> Orchid Soul strongly recommends a trial encounter based on this initial fantasy exchange. If you agree to the encounter, please press the "Agree" button, otherwise select "Cancel." Please note that agreeing to the encounter means revealing your username and e-mail address to your chosen candidate.

Natasha's breath caught in her throat. No. Eileen had said it was all anonymous! Okay, that was definitely a bug . . . or Eileen's idea of a scary joke. She drummed her fingers on the table, trying to decide which.

Unexpectedly a screen popped up a window announcing, "Connection time-out error: 475."

A sudden wave of unexpected tension left her fingers cold as Natasha reached for a nearby writing pad and made some notations for Eileen to fix.

She looked up when the computer beeped. Then, with a blink, it refreshed, announcing, "Thank you for agreeing to continue with Candidate One. Your identities and fantasy entries will be exchanged once he agrees to your profile. We will notify you both via text message."

Natasha stared in shock for a few seconds. That sounded too real. Was it really going to reveal her identity? She grabbed her phone and punched in Eileen's phone number. It sent her to voice mail, so she tried again.

And again.

"Damn." She glared at her phone and bit her lip. Telling herself there was no need to panic yet, Natasha set the phone down.

Well, best-case scenario, this was nothing but a joke taken way too far. In which case, she'd hunt Eileen down and explain the difference between horror and humor.

Worst-case scenario, her first fantasy would go to someone who could identify her, if only via e-mail. She'd have to do some damage control. Hmm, maybe she'd tell her "mate" that it had been for fun—that the system was corrupt and he needed to ignore the whole thing. What was it exactly that she'd written down for her first fantasy anyway?

Ah, yes. Thanks to the conversation with the mysterious nonsmoking stranger, she'd submitted a "sex with a stranger in a stairwell" fantasy. *In a stairwell big enough to be an echo chamber. No questions. No conversation. No strings attached. Just some seriously sweaty sex.*

Okay, so maybe she could chalk that up to courage and conviction, but she was definitely losing points in the clarity and control department. On the other hand, she'd made the statement when she thought her fantasy would be anonymous.

Screw it. If Candidate One was even the slightest bit of a gentleman, he'd realize how embarrassing this could become for both of them and ignore the Orchid Soul messages.

Twenty minutes later, she was finally concentrating on the paperwork in her hands when the gentle chime of her PDA broke into her thoughts.

Congratulations! Candidate One has agree to participate as your mate, so Orchid Soul is advancing your profiles to phase 2.

The identity of Candidate One is: *Mr. Logan Taylor.* Contact information is provided below. We strongly suggest you meet beforehand. On behalf of Orchid Soul, thank you and best of luck.

"Oh. My. God!"

Unbe-fucking-lievable! The attorney in her wanted to rip Eileen a new one. Her mind was spinning with the implications. God, she was going to murder Eileen! She tried in vain to think of Eileen's team of programmers. What were their names? Judy? Sarah? And that red-headed one . . . Anna? Heck, she didn't have their phone numbers, so what difference did it make?

Bolting out of her chair, Natasha paced to her office window, looking out at the setting sun. Below her, commuters were fighting bumper-to-bumper traffic as they headed home, someone leaning heavily on their horn.

The PDA buzzed again, and she rushed back to catch the incoming message. This time it was from "Logan Taylor."

I must've missed the memo that stated this was no longer anonymous. If you'd like to meet, I'll be at the Blue Ring Bistro in an hour, at the table by the window. If you don't show up, I'll understand you do not wish to pursue this.

"Damned straight," she mumbled aloud, still staring at the PDA. She had to put the lockdown on this. No way was she going to let Mr. Taylor think that she wanted to go through with it. It would be best to handle it like any of her cases.

She'd walk in like the power attorney that her mother was. Walk in like she was in control, clear things up with a few sharp, convincing statements, and be done with it in less than ten minutes. Just in time for a nice solo dinner.

Natasha toed her shoes back on, threw a stick of gum into her mouth, and checked her wristwatch, calculating how long it would take her to lock up and make it to the bistro on time.

She had her purse, keys, and briefcase in hand when she paused at the doorway, glanced back to her computer, then returned to it. Anyone who'd ever been born had a profile somewhere on the Internet, and as every attorney knows, knowledge is power. Surely she could get a feel for the kind of person he was in a few minutes. It was as good a place as any.

The name search yielded several different articles that boiled down to three different profiles, as different from one another as could be.

Either Candidate One was a wealthy, powerful business-man, a princely humanitarian . . . or a shady character.

Well, two out of three wasn't bad.

The Blue Ring Bistro was popular for its neo cupcakes, dark ambience, and damn-near-orgasmic coffee. It had taken al-most all of Logan's willpower to give up cigarettes, and if any-one suggested he give up his favorite source of caffeine, he'd without question have to take a life.

From his post by the window, he watched as his not-so-blind date stepped out of her car and headed for the bistro. He knew the reflective glass would make it hard for her to see inside, so he watched the strut of her curvaceous hips and the soft sway of her breasts, femininity all wrapped up in a business suit that spelled trouble. She really was quite a package.

Subtle sexiness. Very effective.

The glower on her face suggested she had a well-rehearsed speech for her "anonymous" date. And given the first impression he'd left with her, he probably deserved it.

Too bad she'd mentioned the stairwell. What an intriguing, uncalculated mistake.

The woman had taken his offhand remark and turned it into one of her fantasies. Into her *first* fantasy, to be precise. A heat of pure satisfaction uncurled in his gut every time he thought of it. How on earth was he supposed to *not* be baited by that?

She entered the bistro and walked directly to the counter, where she placed her order. She put her change back in her wallet, then ever so casually she turned toward his seat at the window—and froze, barely controlled shock washing over her face.

He watched her lips form the word "Fuck," and he couldn't help the visceral satisfaction it brought him.

So, this was Natasha Madison.

He winked, and her gaze narrowed before she abruptly looked away, turning her back to him until her beverage was ready. The view of her butt wasn't bad, so he kept looking, admiring her curves.

She picked up her coffee and approached his table, her face holding on to a stiff smile.

Part of him, the part his grandmother had raised with manners and politeness, wanted to hold the chair for her. But he squelched the impulse.

He wasn't a thug—at least, not anymore. But he sure as hell wasn't going to pretend to be a docile, predictable gentleman either.

So he remained slouched in his chair, his legs stretched out and crossed over at his dusty boots, his half-filled cup of coffee steaming in his hands.

"Well, if it isn't Tasha Madison," he murmured, taking a sip.

"Natasha," she corrected.

She sat poker-straight in the chair across from him and crossed her elegant legs, setting her purse in her lap in a way that indicated she wouldn't stay long. He liked the way her understated fig-brown suit revealed so little of her. A slender ankle, elegant hands, the pearl necklace at her slim neck.

"We meet again, Mr. Taylor," she finally spoke.

"Logan," he corrected in turn.

She took a sip, ignoring the remark. He couldn't remember the last time he'd been so attracted to a woman who looked that conservative. Probably never. He'd always preferred women who were a little rough around the edges. Less soft-spoken. Even physically stronger.

This woman was too . . . soft. Even with her defenses up, she looked too damned vulnerable.

She shifted ever so slightly in her seat and looked at him, her eyes behind her glasses filled with an embarrassed gleam that spelled "hands off."

So why was he fighting the urge to pull her into his lap?

Jesus, she was so goddamned wrong for him.

And vice versa.

And still, he wouldn't mind seeing her lose herself in an

orgasm. One brought on by him. Mmm-mmm-mmm. Sweet Lord . . . He bit back a groan.

Her eyes widened. "Did you just growl?"

He practiced his angelic look. "Growl?"

Her coffee cup paused halfway to her lips. "I thought you—never mind."

He recrossed his legs and waited. Her floral perfume was light and seductive. He preferred musky scents, but this scent worked for her. Her semi-glossy lipstick gleamed in the soft overhead light. Nothing stark for her. Just muted, subtle tones. It started his mind on all kinds of interesting thoughts.

"Mr. Taylor—"

"Logan."

"Of course." Her stiff smile widened just a tad. "Logan, let's cut to the chase, shall we? After our brief and insightful conversation a few days ago, we agreed that we are not in the least compatible. This match that Orchid Soul has cooked up between us is not only flawed but a violation of the privacy we were guaranteed upon participation. Can we agree that this effort is futile and the logical thing to do is delete the e-mails, contact Eileen, and have her deactivate our accounts?"

"I would, but . . . Look, I know our first meeting didn't go so well. I admit I was an ass, but maybe we can start over."

"I think that's exactly why we shouldn't."

He smiled, made sure he caught her eye before asking, "Has Orchid Soul sent you anything of mine yet?"

"No."

Damn. "Want me to spoil it for you?"

Her eyes narrowed a bit. "What's this about?"

"Let's just say I couldn't forget your pearl necklace."

Her eyes widened, disbelief clear on her face. "Why are you telling me this?"

"Because it all comes down to why we're both here. I want to know if you'd seriously consider taking things to the next level."

"The next level?" Her fingers tightened ever so slightly around her coffee mug, but she remained stubbornly silent.

"You submitted a stairwell fantasy, Tasha."

Her reply was almost too neutral, too controlled. "So?"

He sipped his coffee, choosing his words carefully. "Your fantasy wasn't exactly random. And you were very specific in your request. Trench coat, but no shirt. Old jeans . . . boots." He balanced one of his boots on top of the other, drawing her gaze down his legs. They were the same ones he'd worn when they'd met before.

She didn't flinch, but she momentarily glanced away, regret clear in her expression.

"I have to say, you surprised me with the no-talking rule." He paused, taking in the way she sat at the edge of the chair, noticing her pulse at her throat, knowing he had her full attention. "Why not indulge in something a bit more satisfying than cyber sex? No one needs to know but us . . . and I'm really good at keeping secrets."

Her eyes widened and her constipated smile stiffened further. "Are you—? Did you just say what I think—? You are out of your mind."

But even with all the confusion in her eyes, he could see the glimmer of surprise and anticipation that matched his own.

She blinked and whispered, "Are you propositioning me?"

"I'm proposing a flesh-for-fantasy, no-strings-attached encounter, yes."

She frowned. "You can't be serious."

"Why not? Most people never work up the nerve to live the life they fantasize about. I may be egotistical, but you obviously wanted someone like me in your fantasy, and heaven knows I wouldn't mind someone like you in mine. Is it so wrong to act on it?"

The intrigue on her face never quite reached outrage, but she continued to stare at him, looking completely confused. The moment stretched as she struggled to speak her mind.

The last thing he expected was for her to lean back and chuckle. "I can't tell if you're serious or not, Mr. Taylor, but I'm afraid I'll have to decline your offer." She gathered her purse and stood. "And like I said before, please delete any of my Orchid Soul e-mails."

He stood as well, so that they were face to face. He couldn't figure out what it was about her that fired up the hungry sexual beast in him, but whether she knew it or not, she had control of the chains. Damned if he knew why that excited him.

Up close, he could see her eyes dilate just a bit. He could see her pulse racing at her throat, could hear the controlled raggedness in her breathing. But it was the flare of heat in her eyes that pleased him the most.

"I *am* serious. It hinges on you." He took a step back, giving her space. "I'll send you an e-mail stating place and time. It ends only if you don't show up in the stairwell."

Those luscious lips of hers parted as the implications sank in, her face reflecting her astonishment and unmistakable desire. "You think I'd just show up and . . ." She swallowed, her eyes accusing, her cheeks flushed. "You really *are* out of your mind."

"Yeah, more than likely," he agreed.

He picked up his motorcycle helmet next to his chair and walked past her on the way to the door, glancing one last time in her direction before he left.

Two ❦

Natasha rested her head against the pillar in the empty stairwell and wondered if anyone had ever been hospitalized for being too horny. Seriously, she hadn't stopped thinking about sex since that fateful day at the bistro.

With a sigh, she reviewed her Diamond Life theory once more.

Courage. Hell, horniness had taken care of that. Sheesh.

Clarity. True, she wasn't drunk. Wasn't being hasty, although the term was questionable. She knew what she was doing. Sorta.

Conviction. Didn't horniness and lust trump conviction?

Control. Yes! He was certainly right about that. Her choice, even if it felt like madness, felt like she was taking control of the whole not-so-anonymous debacle.

Next to her, the curved stairwell of the high-tech building spiraled down several levels to the main floor.

Even with her eyes shut, she could still see the e-mail Logan had sent:

> Thigh-high nylons. Black high heels. Pearl earrings (no necklace). Leave your hair down. Raincoat, but stay naked underneath. Or surprise me.

She tugged at the belt of her raincoat, damn near hyperventilating. Surprise him? Hell, she was surprising the heck out of herself.

Ten minutes to midnight, and here she was.

Alone.

In a lunar-lit stairwell.

At the moment, all the neon exit signs were beckoning her to escape.

Tipping her head back, she looked up past the glass ceiling, at the sliver of moon that hung like a scythe in the inky sky. It really was a gorgeous stairwell. Fourteen stories tall, echoed like a cave. And by the looks of it, the first two floors were the only ones occupied.

Had she lost her mind? The man was a stranger.

She ought to leave right now! He'd never know.

In a burst of movement, she turned and headed for the door, her heels echoing loudly in the chamber while she quickly pulled her hair up into a tight, simple knot. She was smarter than this! Diamond Life be damned.

This was neither safe nor sane. Although fifteen years of karate had taught her a thing or two about defending herself if it became necessary, this was still dangerous.

With each step, the lining of her raincoat brushed silkily

against her nudity, reminding her she'd gone without sex for way too long. Still, she admitted, the thought of sex with a stranger was the biggest part of the thrill. Nothing sane about that.

Halfway to the door, she stopped.

She'd never come by this kind of insane attraction before. And, strictly speaking, he was a fine physical specimen to have sex with. This was as far into the wild side as she was ever going to get. A once-in-a-lifetime kind of thing. And he had exactly two minutes before she chickened out completely.

She turned on her heel and with slower steps returned to the pillar. So . . .

Hell, maybe he'd staged this to teach her a lesson in humility.

She closed her eyes and sighed, but a quiet click had her opening them again, the sound echoing in the chamber.

Suddenly, there he was, the door closing silently behind him.

Natasha barely realized she was holding her breath.

His trench coat showed off his broad shoulders, the front hanging open just enough to reveal his naked chest. He seemed even taller than she'd remembered, but maybe it was his black boots and black jeans that gave that illusion.

The perfect stranger . . .

Logan's gaze held hers so intimately, she felt stripped by him. Desire fired in her blood like a flame to gasoline, making it utterly impossible to look away. His head full of braids made him look wild, untamed, and more than a little dangerous.

Natasha's heart thundered in her chest, all but echoing in the chamber with every step that he took as he approached her. She thought she'd been prepared for what to expect, but the emotions of arousal and danger running through her were too raw, making her lean heavily against the wall.

She opened her mouth to speak, to voice her anxieties, but a quick shake of his head kept the words unspoken.

No talking. Why on earth had she ever written that into her fantasy to begin with? Her breathing deepened, each quiet exhale audible in the stillness of the chamber.

For an endless moment, she was trapped by his gaze, pleading for an understanding she couldn't explain, studying the passionate intent in his dark eyes that seemed to pull her even closer to him.

Two slow steps and he was finally in front of her, inches separating them, her eyes at his cheek level. The clean scent of his clothes and body heat were accented by his mild, slightly citrusy cologne.

His hands came up and she held perfectly still, shuddering just a little as they slid over her hair, loosening the bun until it cascaded to her shoulders.

His low hum vibrated into the silence like a primitive growl, drawing a tingling response all the way from her toes. But he moved his hands to the wall beside her head and waited.

The next move was hers.

Time seemed to compress into itself as she fought with the tiny voices of decency and reason that struggled inside her. She should shove him away and head out the door! She wasn't really going to get intimate with a man she hardly knew, was she? She should laugh it off. His ego could handle it.

One by one, the arguments muted, until they faded to a tiny whimper.

Logan was giving her the fantasy if she wanted it.

And God, she wanted! Blindly. Illogically.

Wanted him!

Her hands faltered just a bit when she reached out and parted his trench coat, little by little, revealing the shadowy span of his bare chest to the faint moonlight.

Despite the cold night outside, he was warm to the touch, almost hot. His lean, clustered muscles tensed as he reacted to the contact. Her mouth watered as, ever so slowly, her fingertips traced the width of his chest, over the heat of his defined abs, while his breathing got noticeably heavier.

Incredible . . .

She licked her lips and spread her fingers, enjoying the sinewy flex in his tensing muscles as she grew bolder, relaxing into the seduction, daring to explore it all over again, memorizing places to kiss. . . .

After the third exploration, she slid her hand toward the topmost button of his jeans.

God, it all felt so surreal.

The front of his jeans strained with the bulge of his erection. She stared, blinked twice, then dared to reach out and verify if the whole, thick length was all him.

Logan inhaled sharply and several of his braids swung forward, brushing her cheek when he moved his groin against her hand in a needy thrust. His low groan sounded both helpless and predatory, arousing her even more.

Sweet Jesus, it was all him! All nice, thick, hard, manly cock. . . .

All hers!

A wet yearning clutched and trembled deep in her womb

and she swallowed dryly, stroking him again, blindly familiar-izing herself with his width, sliding lower to cup his balls through the soft jeans before stroking him again.

Another primitive moan rumbled in his chest, and his head lowered as if her touch was torturing him, until his warm breath brushed her cheek. Pure instinct had her turning her face, her lips sensitive to his barely bristly jaw, placing the first kiss there.

For a moment, it seemed like time stalled and stretched in endless milliseconds while their gazes locked.

The raw desire in Logan's eyes smoldered, openly daring her to do more. Licking her lips, Natasha stroked the bulge of his jean-clad cock again. He moved against the contact, once . . . twice . . . then groaned, lowered his face into the nape of her neck and sank his teeth ever so gently in a soft, spine-tingling love bite.

She gasped, sliding on the sensation as his tongue flicked out over the bite, the heat of his lips and mouth moving up her neck, over her cheek, the sounds of each suckle and jagged breath raiding her senses.

She'd just gasped in air when he sealed his mouth over hers, his lips taking hers in a devouring kiss that ruthlessly sucked the breath from her lungs, devastating and lustful, leaving her feeling deliciously weak and dizzy. And severely horny.

A corner of her mind realized that the pornographic moans echoing through the chamber had come from her.

He tasted of cool mint chocolate, making her want to rav-ish his mouth again until she fainted. He angled for more, his lips and tongue expertly and intimately taking her breath away.

God, he was good at that!

Lost in the sensation of his tongue, she greedily eased against him, barely remembering to steal more air before drowning under another kiss . . . and another. . . .

His groans vibrated against her mouth, humming deep inside her, tightening in her breasts, pooling in her belly, seducing her without words.

Everywhere she turned her head, his mouth followed, demanding, his tongue engaging hers with a skill that made her pussy tingle with anticipation. When he finally buried his face against her jaw, she shuddered and involuntarily moaned weakly, overwhelmed by the desperate need to have him deeply buried inside her.

As if she'd spoken her thoughts, he eased back marginally, his face still inches from hers, the absence of his body heat sobering her with unwanted logic.

Moving his hands from next to her head, he gripped the belted knot of her coat and in a single tug, had it undone. She tensed, becoming unexpectedly apprehensive.

The coat belt slipped from his fingers and he parted her coat slowly, as if he had all the time in the world, and with a reverence that made her toes curl. His breathing became more ragged and the sound he made of pure male appreciation had her squeezing her thighs together to hold back the instant wet response.

She watched, fascinated, aware that she was fully revealed, in a way she'd never been for any other man. She stood there, proudly showing off the thigh-high black nylons, her carefully trimmed pussy, her full, aroused breasts. She'd dusted glimmer sugar powder on her nipples earlier and was glad to see him fascinated by the fact.

Surprise!

His angular face tightened with desire and saw the flare of his nostrils as he continued to look his fill. His hand remained at her waistline, possessively, stretching out the moment.

He nudged his right boot between her heeled shoes, spreading her legs just a few inches, then he closed his eyes and inhaled the scent of her obvious arousal, groaning as if he was imagining his nose nuzzling her clit.

Natasha swallowed audibly, thirstily, making a sound that bordered on a helpless whimper. Her eyes opened, then he lowered his head until his mouth touched her left breast, his lips suckling the aroused nipple that seemed to tug the G-spot deep in her gut. She almost squirmed, arching against him when the suction became a taut, delicious, love bite.

His hands went to the tops of her nylons, rimming the edge inward, to her inner thighs, trailing back out and around to the back, where he cupped her buttocks in his hands.

She was past caring what she sounded like when his fingertips trailed up to her quivering belly, then delved down steadily between her thighs again. She was dying for him to hurry up, but his pace remained infuriatingly slow and steady.

He slid two fingers against her clit, teasing with the slick wetness that had pooled at the folds of her pussy.

As his hot mouth abraded her breast, his fingers dipped further, their long, insistent pressure completely exploring her vagina even as his booted feet mutely commanded her to widen her stance. Her breast ached with fullness, his mouth ravishing every part until she was almost weeping, wordlessly pleading for more.

He switched to her other breast and flicked a tongue around

her nipple just as a single finger slid wetly, deeply into her pussy, causing her to shudder and lock her knees to keep standing.

"Oh God! Oh . . . f-fuck!" Her whispers broke from her lips as she ground her hips against his skillful hand. Her mouth hung open as she rode the first spike of pleasure that normally preceded most of her orgasms.

"Shh . . ." He punished her nipple with a soft bite and his mouth covered hers just as his hand shifted again, pushing two fingers into her, his thumb nestling against the ridge of her swollen clit.

A strangled moan choked in her throat, but she responded on instinct, grinding against his clever touch again . . . once, then twice, gritting her teeth to contain the unraveling pleasure.

Goddamn, that felt good!

He nuzzled her ear, nibbled it, found her pearl earring and flicked his tongue around the orb, teasing it in an oral kiss that almost made her come on the spot.

"Oh! . . ." She shifted, trying to get away from the sensual assault, but failed. Knowing she wasn't going to be able to hold back if he kept going, she shook her head, mutely trying to warn him.

But still he kept his mouth against her ear, her neck, her cheek, his hands finger-stroking her as if he'd done it his whole life. Deliriously on edge, she could hardly think as her impending orgasm wound tighter, building with every finger thrust, encroaching like a bubbling storm inside her.

Their echoes of desire blended and whispered together in the chamber, growing choppier with each rough breath. The hushed contact of their clothes added to the mix.

When she least expected it, he removed his hand, wiping his dripping knuckles against her clit before pushing her higher against the pillar from where she'd been steadily slipping.

Natasha sagged against it, struggling to find her sanity as he pushed back his coat, reached for the zipper of his jeans, and tugged it down to reveal his erection.

It was mesmerizing, watching that beautiful cock as if it was a present. It jutted out firm and thick, with the scent of aroused musky maleness. In less than two seconds, he was sliding a condom on.

Good God!

There was a quivering strain in her belly, and for the first time, she worried that he might be too much. He was certainly bigger than any past lover.

In Logan's face was pure male intent—he was a man aroused and on the edge. She licked her lips, wanting to beg him to hurry. To fill her. To fuck her. Hard. Solid!

Now!

He tugged his jeans down lower, grabbing his cock and stroking it, the lingering wetness from her pussy gleaming on his hand against the condom. She reached for it, pushed her pussy against it, guiding it to her. *Goddammit, do me! Hurry!*

He ravaged her mouth with a hard kiss before pushing his sheathed cock into her vagina.

"Oh!" Finally! Fuck! Oh, God . . . Oh, God . . . sweet . . . so, oh, ohh . . . fuckin' deep . . .

He flexed his hips and the rest of his cock filled her, sheathing snugly within her. She forgot to breathe as her sex adjusted like a hungry mouth. A bead of sweat rolled down his cheek when he kissed her softly, tongued her bottom lip, and flexing again, locked the thick inches of his cock into her so completely that she could hardly suppress the exquisite shudder.

He held still, controlling the movement. Their bellies touched together with each jagged breath. His hands went to her hips and lifted her more securely against the pillar. She wrapped her legs around him, and the readjustment shifted his cock higher, easily targeting her ever-elusive G-spot.

Oooooooh!

His mouth tangled with hers, starting a rhythm of a good, solid, friction-filled stroke . . . then easing out just enough to make them both groan before doing it all over again.

She moaned and clutched his shoulders, undulating her hips and feeling his cock aim true to her quiver zone. She kissed him harder, becoming desperate with need, demanding and taking, ordering him without words to take on a faster pace.

They spoke in grunts, hungry kisses, and urging bites. She blindly nuzzled and licked his neck, sucked his skin, and shifted her hips again when he rocked with more slow-paced strokes.

His hiss of breath warmed her ear, his teeth clicked against the pearl earring there, and with the next inhale, he surged into her again, their bodies trembling with thin, unraveling control.

Please, oh, please . . . She muffled her cries against his cheek. Again and again, her pussy choked and clenched with juicy pleasure.

They moved as if pushed together, his whole body rubbing hers, his cock rammed so perfectly against her G-spot that she felt each grind of his pelvis against her clit.

The unexpected rush of pleasure sizzled over so suddenly

she couldn't prepare for the flash that unleashed deep inside, sending ripples of shameless shivers all the way through to her toes, her nipples aching, the air against her lips sizzling like static. She cried out, surrendering to it completely.

Behind her eyes, she was hurled into the orgasm . . . unbreathing and blind.

The muscles of her pussy gripped and clenched around him in several hard spasms, riding the crashing waves of sharp-spiked pleasure. His arms clenched harder around her, his pounding rhythm becoming more urgent.

With no time to muffle her cries, the second orgasm tore from her throat, flooding the stairwell with her broken moans of surprise and release, of his grunts and wet thrusts that surged over and over against that magic spot in her womb. She grabbed his braids in her fists and begged brokenly into his ear.

"Please . . . fuck . . . God . . ."

Whatever control he had left snapped. He surged again, ejaculating deep inside her, thick and hot. He braced himself and shuddered hard against her, hot inside her, tightly embracing her. His moans lingered with hers in the orgylike echoes of the chamber.

He kept moving in and out of her, slowing, like defective machinery that had to be unplugged to bring it to a stop. Her vagina hummed with sensitivity, and it was all she could to do to hold on to his shoulders and sag against the pillar, enduring the lovely, melting aftershocks.

The curtain of his hair braids provided a haven for her face to rest, isolating the distinct scent of him, his trench coat, and his cologne into her every breath.

Good Lord. That had been insanely good.

Mind-numbing, clit-shuddering, incredibly good.

Insane.

Jesus H. Christ, she'd just had sex with a stranger.

She turned to see that his eyes were halfway open, watching her, his chest still billowing. Knowing the magic would soon end, she tugged a handful of his braids, lowering his mouth to hers.

The kiss was long and lazy, pure mutual satisfaction.

One hand trailed over her cheek, making her aware that he wasn't the only one who was perspiring.

They remained that way for what seemed like forever, his cock not quite returning to limpness inside her. He carefully placed playful little kisses on her cheek, the tender act causing emotion to well in her throat.

She couldn't hold back the flinch when she tried to shift her weight and her thighs trembled. A frown furrowed his brow and he eased out of her, setting her feet gingerly on the ground.

Trickles of wetness began sliding down her thighs, stopping at the mid-thigh nylons.

God, she ought to get a mold of that impressive cock and custom-make a dildo. Or a million of them. If it didn't bring world peace, the dildo would at least bring a wide, satisfied smile to women everywhere. Surely that would count for something.

Except, she realized with a sudden vengeance, she wanted his cock to be hers. Exclusively hers.

And she wanted to play with him again.

His intense gaze warmed, the mystery in his eyes telling her nothing and yet holding none of his satisfaction back. Finally, he pulled up his jeans, tucking his lovely, world-peace-nominated cock back and zipping up.

Feeling self-conscious, Natasha pulled her raincoat closed, pressing her thighs together to hold the lingering sensations at bay.

An awkward silence threatened to swamp them.

A flicker of mischief ghosted over his eyes, but he seemed hesitant about something, and if she didn't know better, he looked almost uncomfortable for about half a second. When she frowned in question, he put his hand on the ledge of the pillar behind her, extracting something metallic, no bigger than a stick of gum.

He carefully placed it into her coat pocket, then leaned toward her and kissed her one final time, hard and possessive.

Only then did he close his trench coat, his final statement a brief, erotic hum of satisfaction. It felt like a spell that wrapped itself around her, inside her, pulsing there long after he'd left.

Three ❧

It was several minutes later when Natasha had finally snapped out of the magical spell that had left her limp and languid against the stairwell. She reached into her pocket to discover that the tiny object he'd put into her pocket was a micro-recorder.

One click replayed the intimate, echoing sounds of the illicit affair: every one of her uncontained moans, every one of his gut-tingling, tremulous grunts, of her begging and cursing, of his hushed whispers and fabric-rustling caresses. It was sharply embarrassing to hear her own orgasm pouring from the tiny device.

She clicked it off.

"Oh, hell." The words echoed around her, filled with surprise and shock.

Disbelief turned into anger and began to twist inside her.

Was this an attempt at blackmail? Seriously? What other motive could he possibly have?

The questions bounced back and forth in her mind, gathering force. She pushed herself from the pillar, straightened her coat and tightened her belt. Had this been a setup?

The deep sexual satisfaction gradually drained, leaving behind nothing but self-anger and regret. If Mr. Logan Taylor was trying to blackmail her, he sure as hell had another thing coming.

It was well past midnight when Logan finally turned his bedside lamp on, feeling only half-awake.

He'd been tossing in his bed, kicking the covers to his feet despite the chill in the air. His cock had remained speared toward the ceiling, impervious to the temperature, the wet dream still as fresh and flushed as the pulse on his erection.

Christ!

And it was all thanks to her damned pearl earrings.

In his dream, he'd all but tasted the one on her right earlobe, rolling it with his tongue. Except it had blurred and shifted, turning into the gentle white clink of her teeth grazing his in an urgent kiss . . . then blurring again, darkening with shadows to become her perky nipple, a delicate black pearl, so real under his mouth, he swore he'd tasted her skin. Finally it changed again and he saw it nestled among blooming lavender petals. He'd dived in, nuzzling and licking it as it became her clit.

That's how he'd woken up with his cock in his hand, his heart in his throat, and Tasha's breathy, pleading gasps still echoing in his ears.

Fuck . . .

Grabbing some tissue nearby, he wiped the remaining cum that trailed over his belly just as his phone chirped to life.

A hundred bucks said it was her.

He checked the alarm clock. One fifty-seven.

So, she'd been able to hold off for a couple of hours before resorting to calling him up. Hell, he shouldn't have slipped her the microrecorder. It seemed like a good idea at the time.

He reached for the phone. "Hello?"

"What do you want, Mr. Taylor? What is the meaning of this device? Blackmail?" Natasha's calm tone didn't fool him one bit.

"No."

"Then what exactly is this?"

He didn't pretend not to understand. "A gift."

"*Gift*?" The word dripped with disbelief.

He studied his ceiling. "From the moment I read your fantasy, I kept thinking about it. Some people have photographic memories. I remember sounds . . . in detail. All I need to do is think back to where I was, and I can remember every breath you made, every moan. . . ."

She seemed to hold her breath before she exhaled in confusion.

"Why should I suffer alone?" he said, only half teasing.

"I'm used to flowers, or a box of candy, or—"

"Look, you're reading too much into it. It's not that complicated," he said. "It's just a gift. That's it. No gimmicks. No blackmail. Just me, and my mad gift-challenged skills."

He waited, surprised by the wisp of dread forming in his gut. It was easy to imagine her tucking a lock of hair behind her ear as she made up her mind. "No more surprises, okay?"

He flashed back to the moment he'd opened the door to find her standing there, waiting for him. Man, what a surprise. "Answer me this. Did you listen to it?"

She fumbled her reply. "A little."

"The whole thing?"

"No."

Liar. "Did you like it?"

This time her pause was longer. "My point is no more gifts. Good night."

She hung up before he could reply.

Four ❦

Please rank the experience of your first encounter with your candidate.

The following morning, Natasha's computer beeped with the incoming Orchid Soul message. She blinked at it, waiting for the caffeine to kick in so she could make sense of the sentence.

Candidate? Shouldn't that say lover? Christ, he'd skillfully fucked her until her toes had tingled. Then she'd shamelessly listened to the recording of it while trying not to feel like a porn addict.

God, the man was arrogant as hell, but there was no denying Logan deserved a friggin' medal—with an enthusiastic thumbs up!

No way in hell was she actually going to score him with perfect high scores. Maybe she'd give him a seven or an eight.

With the bugs in the system, there was always a chance he could find out what she'd graded him and then what? She chucked her tongue. His ego would expand and require its own zip code.

Thinking for a moment, she set her coffee mug down. On the other hand, what had he rated her? Would she get to find out how he scored her?

Worried that if she waited too long, the defective system would decide for her, she hurriedly scored a seven but didn't feel much relief at the polite "Thank you" that followed.

It could've meant "Thank you. We're now calculating your score in complete anonymous confidentiality," or "Thank you. We're about to let the entire world know that you scored your lover a measly seven points."

Either way, it was too late to make any changes now.

Much later, well into her second cup of coffee, she got the next e-mail.

> Your candidate found you to be compatible and ranked your first encounter as: "highly satisfactory." Per your scoring, he has been advised your past encounter: "could use improvement" in order to achieve a higher level of satisfaction for you . . .

Oh, sweet God. She groaned, rubbing her forehead. *Could use improvement?* What had she done? Her eyes scanned the rest of the message for the last line.

> His fantasy is: *Pearls at the pool hall.*

She'd been staring at the words for a while before Logan's e-mail appeared on the screen.

> Okay, lover, let's step it up then. Wear high heels and your favorite little black dress. Low cut. Garters. Show up at the address below at 10:00 p.m. and don't be late.

She could practically hear his gravelly voice reading off each request. Calmly. Seductively. A devil full of that infernal wickedness that made her knees weak.

The pit of her stomach clenched, the intimate quiver of anticipation causing her to place a covering hand over her belly. She swiveled her chair away to stare out the window.

If this was control, it sure didn't feel like it. It felt like chaos, reckless and exciting, becoming a growing anticipation that had her catching her breath.

Who knew pearls and pool halls went together?

Since the address was at the heart of historic Sacramento, the location wasn't hard to find. It was certainly not on the main side of town that she usually visited. In fact, she hadn't known that the alleyway was even there.

The path to Bruno's Pub and Brew was well lit, but the cobblestone path was hell on her shoes. A handful of chrome-gilded motorcycles marked the entrance, and a quiet, steady trickle of water identified a pipe leak somewhere nearby. Two low-level male voices were barely louder than the thump of hard music blasting like a frightened heartbeat from somewhere inside. She had to squint at the shapes under the awning to make out the profile of Logan's braided head as he leaned against the wall by the door. Next to him, a muscular man crushed his cigarette under his heel, shared some sort of secret handshake with Logan, then headed inside.

Logan pushed off the wall and stood waiting for her. She had the feeling he'd sensed her before she'd seen him.

"Sexy," he said, as she approached. A gnawed swizzle stick stuck out like a mangled toothpick from between his lips as his grin widened. "You're late."

She stopped an arm's length away from him, feeling herself sinking into the forbidden role of mystery lover. "And you've been shamelessly sucking up secondhand smoke."

"Guilty." He grinned and tossed the swizzle stick into the cigarette bin. "I've got my weaknesses."

She glanced around. "So, you work here or something?"

"Something like that. Nice pearls."

"Thanks." She briefly ran the tips of her fingers over them, absurdly pleased when his eyes followed the movement. Man, how did he do that? How did he make her feel naked except for the pearls?

"Mr. Taylor—"

"Call me Logan. And I'll call you Tasha."

Tasha from the stairwell, she thought. Tasha, the horny, mysterious stranger who really, really wanted to cop a feel all over his fine self. Damn . . .

"Okay," she agreed, finally tearing her gaze away from him to look around. "So, did you want to stand here, or . . ."

He stepped closer, cupped her face in his hands, and, waiting just a millisecond to hold her gaze, lowered his head toward hers.

Just that quick glimpse of the desire in his eyes had her breath trembling on her lips before he covered them with his. It was devastating how quickly his kiss could make her so senseless, so immediately yearning and breathless. Instinctively, she clutched his shirt right above his belt buckle and held on. She melted under the single-minded way his mouth ate her up as if she'd gobbled up the world's last piece of chocolate.

After what felt like an eternity, his head lifted, and he nipped her swollen lips gently.

And it wasn't nearly enough, she realized. Not by a long shot.

"Do you know how to play pool?" he asked, his voice gruff and deep.

Natasha struggled to understand him, then licked her lips and tried to talk herself out of jumping his cock right on the spot. "Um, I've played once. Long ago."

He stepped back, his eyes making her feel decadently naked. "Let's see what you know."

She caught herself tightening the belt of her coat as he put his arm loosely around her shoulder and led her into the loud bar. It was a dark den with carefully placed lighting that showcased the long bar as well as the corner stage where a bluesy rock band was playing. Behind the bar, huge shiny vats glistened, and she realized that the predominant smell of hops meant this was a real brewery.

"Want anything to drink?" he murmured against her ear.

"An apple martini," she murmured back.

He raised an eyebrow in amusement.

What? Too sissy? "A cosmopolitan?" she amended.

His lips twitched into a faint smile. "How about a Long Island iced tea?"

"Sure."

Like vampires clad in leather, the clientele clustered around barstools and tall tables. She squinted at a few of them, suddenly realizing that she was looking at a few celebrities. Or was she? The lighting was too obscure to tell.

Over the noise, she didn't hear what Logan ordered, but less than a minute later, the bartender slid the drinks over to them.

Logan's hand lowered to the back of her spine as he led her through the room, nodding his acknowledgments with his trademark smile. Just when she thought he was heading for a corner, the dim light revealed an adjacent pool den where several people were playing.

One table lay undisturbed, waiting for them.

Never would she have come to a bar like this on her own, she admitted to herself. It both embarrassed and worried her that she was getting a rush from the experience now.

But she felt safe.

Logan led her to one of the corner tables, where it seemed even darker than the rest of the room. She settled gingerly on the edge of the stool, sipped her strong drink, and watched the pool game in progress, feeling very much like an outsider as she listened to the friendly yet edgy banter among the players.

"Take off your coat." Logan's gaze locked with hers, daring her to defy his request.

She shrugged it off her shoulders, setting it against the back of her tall bar stool. The warmth of the coat had intensified her perfume a bit more, but she felt colder without it. Despite the shadows, she watched Logan's gaze lower to her cleavage, pausing there just a spell before going all the way down to mid-thigh, where her little black dress ended. She wondered if he could see the black seam of her garter belt.

"Ladies first," he said, with a wave of his hand toward the waiting billiards table.

She stood, feeling the heat of alcohol stirring up her passion. She brushed her body against his and boldly dropped a faint kiss against his lips. Before she could move away, his arm wrapped around her waist and he deepened the kiss, revving up the heat to dangerous levels.

By the time they broke apart, she was gulping in air and trying to pretend she hadn't forgotten there were others in the room. If they were alone, she would've easily gone down on him. Hell, she wanted to grope him as it was.

Because the dress had somehow shifted too high up for her comfort, she straightened it and tugged down at the hem before sashaying over to the cues on the table and selecting one. She could feel Logan prowling behind her and around to the other side of the table as she chalked the tip.

She bent over, damn near pushing her cleavage against the felt of the table as she aimed at the triangular cluster of balls.

"Enjoying the view?" she asked quietly.

"Tremendously." He moved closer, just enough to lean toward her. "You should play this naked for me sometime."

"With pearls, of course."

"Goes without saying."

She took aim and let loose, the clash of balls breaking randomly over the felt.

Logan tsked and moved to stand behind her. "Your aim needs work. You have to rock it first, see if you have enough friction for the cue to slide, to control the speed of the hit."

His body pressed against her and his hand covered hers, demonstrating his point. Natasha felt as if the sounds in the room had become more muffled. There seemed to be only his body heat and his words.

"Easy as pie," she replied, somewhat breathily.

"Like sex. It's all about the rocking motion, the friction, the angle, and the slide. But the most important part, of course, is the final hit. There's nothing quite like getting one in the pocket, don't you think?"

Yup! Instead she glanced back at him. "Stop breathing down my neck and let me play."

He chuckled but moved, his hand lingering ever so briefly to where her dress met her thigh. Then he sauntered to the opposite side of the table again.

And so it began.

He played an excellent, calculated game, and there was no doubt in her mind he deliberately botched his turns just so he could see her bent over the table more often. And although she was craving his kiss, he barely touched her—a hand resting momentarily on her hips, or a discreet kiss on her shoulder, or a quick cop of her butt.

The alcohol was definitely kicking in. She felt warmer, friskier, and found herself fighting the urge to run her hands over his body or flip him on the table to get freaky. She wanted to feel the length of his sex in her palm again.

Finally, she simply grabbed him by his braids and kissed him hard and long, not caring who watched. Logan broke away long enough to replace their cue sticks and led her back to their table, easing her further into the corner to take up where they'd left off.

Even though they were tucked in the depths of the shadowy corner, she could sense the others glancing in their direction, but God, she didn't care. Logan's mouth nuzzled her jaw, her ear, devoured her mouth, while his right hand, hidden from view, began to lift the hem of her dress.

Sobriety seeped in like drops of cold water. It was one thing to make out like a teenager, but this? "What are you doing?" she managed.

He nipped her kiss-puffed lower lip. "Stepping it up a notch. Don't move."

She stiffened, embarrassed and yet unable to look away as his hand slid into her thong underwear. Into the moist, lubricated wetness of her arousal. His mouth covered hers just as the sweet contact of his fingertips rubbed over her clit.

God! Oh, fuck, fuck, fuck . . .

"Easy, babe," he murmured against her mouth. "Easy."

She was breathing in gasps by the time she heard the tiny snap. Seconds later, she felt the tiny buttonlike device that nestled against her clitoris, against where his fingers were stroking her, damn near making her moan like a woman in labor.

"Christ, what are you doing?" she asked, more than a little concerned.

"I know how much you love surprises, so I got you a new toy . . . with remote-control access." A lipstick-sized device appeared briefly in his hand. "I think you'll like it."

With a twist, the tiny gadget he'd pinned to the front of her thong began to vibrate against her aroused clit, silently wringing out the most pleasurable sensation without a sound.

"Holy . . ." Shit! A tiny vibrator. Sweet God. "No!" she whispered. "That's not fair!"

He sucked gently on her neck. "Never," he licked, "ever," he sucked, "expect me to play fair."

Her mind was still sluggish when he tugged the hem of her dress back down.

His voice rumbled by her ear. "I like the garters, by the way. Very sexy."

He kissed her hard, silencing her weak moan. Through the onslaught of tingles, she felt the ridge of his erection against her thigh and rocked against it.

"Pace yourself," he said, his gruff voice getting even more gravelly. "You have to sink seven balls before I turn this toy off."

"You've got to be kidding me."

His grin was downright wicked. "Am I?" He stepped away from her, just an arm's length. "But there's one little catch."

"Um, other than the fact that I'm riding the world's tiniest cyclone?" Her heart was thundering, and all that kissing now made her feel like she was running a fever.

He chuckled. "No."

Out of his back pocket, he pulled out a piece of cloth that he unraveled to reveal a scarf. "You play blindfolded."

She meant to laugh, but could only stare.

"Don't worry. I'll guide you."

The vibrator made it hard to even express her disbelief. "You're insane."

"My rules. My game."

In a flash, he'd half-turned her and had the soft scarf over her eyes. It felt like cotton rather than silk, and she reached for it, but he stopped her. A short moment later, he had the blindfold secured and turned her to face him again, kissing her briefly once again on the lips.

"Let's see how you follow orders," he murmured, taking her hand in his.

"If we're ever to get along, you'll learn that I don't do orders."

"Even if I ask nicely?"

"You ask nicely?"

She felt his lips on her shoulder. "For this, I will."

She hesitated, resisted. "How about we do this in a more private setting?" Maybe it was her imagination, but she felt as if there was a sudden shift of mood in the room. Was everyone going to be watching her?

"This is as private as it gets." He tugged her hand again and she followed, trying with all her power to ignore the mini-humming against her clit.

Every step seemed like it was in slow motion, jiggling her cleavage, swaying in her hips—and it sure felt as if the whole world was watching her every move. It was dumb. And dangerous.

And such an unexpected thrill!

She tried to settle her breathing, but it was too erratic. Why on earth was she so aroused by the thought of the other players watching her?

"Here's the table," he finally spoke. "And here's your cue stick."

He placed it into her hand.

"Logan, this is not my thing."

"Shh." He moved behind her, barely touching, his breath by her ear. "I don't give a damn about the others in this room. I just want to watch you play pool. I'm selfish. This is for no one else but me. So, play."

"I don't think I can," she said.

"Come on, Sexy," he coaxed with that tempting voice of his. She felt his kiss on the slope of her shoulder, as his hand slid over the side of her hip. "Bend over . . . I'll help you set up your shot."

"I'll just bet you will," she murmured under her breath, only to be tortured by a quick spike in the vibrator's humming before he turned it down again. She hissed in air, hearing him already moving away from her.

"Go ahead," he said. "I'll be at the other side of the table."

Except she sensed that he hadn't moved a muscle. She leaned forward, bent low, and hoped to God that her garters weren't showing. Okay, maybe just a little.

With every breath, her breasts all but rubbed against the felt of the pool table, and the weight of the pearls felt like his touch against her skin. There was definite tension in the air, and she knew she somehow commanded it.

Licking her lips, she took blind aim, hearing Logan move just when she was about to shoot.

"Wait. Aim for my voice."

She angled a bit to the left.

"Hmm. Nice." She'd bet her paycheck he was staring right at her cleavage again. "More."

She bent lower, pushing her breasts to the table, but not changing her aim one bit.

"Perfect."

In the background the music had become a slow guitar riff that thumped through her blood. Voices murmured in the periphery. Her hand tightened around the cue.

Slide it, he'd said.

Friction, he'd said.

Get the hit.

The fucking vibrator was making her wet, craving his hard, thrusting friction, and ultimate hit.

"Shoot."

She did. There was the telltale clicking sound of two balls colliding, then the quiet swoosh of one falling into the pocket.

She smiled.

There was a low rumble of voices in approval, validating her suspicion that people really were watching her. She straightened, feeling self-conscious.

"Six to go," Logan spoke at her left. When had he moved?

With his hand at her spine, he walked her a few steps around the corner of the table. "This one is closer. Don't lean in too far."

She waited to hear him move away from her. He didn't.

She bent and her hand accidentally touched one of the billiards on the table.

"You're okay. Just don't move from there."

She froze in place, because she suddenly felt the vibrator rev up even more just before his arms braced on either side of her hips. Instead of feeling embarrassed, she had the strongest urge to grind her butt against his cock.

"Looks to me like you're already dead center," he said from somewhere over her right shoulder. "Go for it."

She almost did. Damned, if she didn't almost grind hard against him, but the tiny voice of reason in her voice sobered her enough to hold back.

"You're crowding me," she said under her ragged breath.

"I want to crowd you much more than this."

"Then let's stop this and go crowd each other some other place," she hissed back.

"You and your need for instant gratification," he rumbled in amusement. "I've got to teach you some self-control."

Well, shit, her self-control was being torn to shreds with every passing second!

"Tasha, unless you are trying to use your psychic powers on the ball, it is just not going to move on its own."

Once again, she shot blindly, but even though she made contact, she didn't hear a pocket shot.

"Missed by a hair."

No! "Damn." She meant it more than he knew.

"Try it again."

Oh, hell no! It would take all night and by then she'd be a weeping, dripping, orgasmic fool! In public, no less.

Acting quickly, she slid the cue stick onto the table until it lay flat, then rolled it all the way to the left then to the right until she heard the sounds of billiard balls fall into several of the pockets.

There was a momentary pause before she heard chuckles and applause from the unseen audience.

Logan's own chuckle rumbled against her spine, full of admiration. "Oh, you're good. More than six in at one time."

He leaned back enough for her to straighten and turn.

In. Oh, yes. She wanted to feel that motion something bad. Her clit was plenty stimulated, her sex was all but purring, and that tiny vibrator had her thighs quivering.

Was he just going to play with the damn remote control all night, or was he going to give her some honest to goodness *fucking sex*? It was scandalous how urgently she needed him inside her aching pussy.

Natasha groped her way from his chest to his face, then kissed him. Hard. The sounds of fading applause turned into hoots and whistles. Logan's hands clamped around her hips, but he kept kissing her where she would've stopped.

"Enough," she finally gasped, glad she was wearing the blindfold. "I came, I played pool, now . . . Oh, actually, I haven't come yet."

Why didn't he turn the damned thing down? She was just too close to losing it. She leaned into his ear, torturing herself just a tiny bit more. "I *need* to fuck! If you are not available for fucking in the next ten seconds, I swear to God, I'll screw the first man I find."

"Then allow me." The snarl set her blood on fire.

Suddenly, they were moving. He took her hand and he led her at a hurried pace from the room, the orgasm so close, she almost wept.

"God," she managed in a desperate whisper, "if you want me to walk, turn off the damn vibrator."

It became blessedly still, although her pussy was wet and quivering. She kept the blindfold on, aware only that they passed several light sources. She could hear the echoing of a hallway and the music becoming just a bit more distant.

She reached for the blindfold but he stopped her. "Where are we going?"

"Trust me."

"Why should I?"

He stopped, the echo of their ragged breaths giving her a flashback to the stairwell. "I can take you back, or you can trust me and come wherever I plan to take you. Make your choice."

I just want sex! she was dying to yell at him. *Now! Here!* But part of her—the reckless, blindfolded part of her—wanted to trust him. She could sense him watching her, and by the tension of his hand in hers, he was anticipating rejection.

"Take me then," she finally said.

They went through several pathways, one right, one left, and into another turn that led down some short spiral steps to a cold damp hallway, before he finally pulled her into a room.

Two seconds after the door was open, she found herself against it, Logan's mouth devouring hers, heard a quick fumble of his belt and what she assumed was the rip of a condom packet. Then she was lifted against the door, her thong tugged aside.

"Oh, God . . . Yes, yes, yes . . . Logan!"

She almost melted in the glorious moment when Logan's hard and thick erection slid with such sweet friction deep into her vagina, nailing the chaotic sensations with a single thrust that felt as if it fused them together.

Behind her eyes, the glow of ecstasy imploded and sizzled all the way to her nipples and toes like electricity, unleashing her orgasm before his second thrust.

"Ooooh!" The sound was torn from her as she bucked into the next wave, clutching him deep inside, tensing and weakening at the same time while the smaller, follow-up orgasms took over without mercy.

And it wasn't over. Not with him still thrusting, grinding, and unbraiding her already sensitive climax.

His body tensed, and within the grip of her body, his cock twitched and lodged deeper, dragging a low, gravelly grunt from him, throwing them both hard against the door one final time, the air quaking like an ocean around them. She felt as if she'd been struck by soft lightning and she rode the sensation, arching as her muscles spasmed.

Incredible . . .

The thought floated in the air, nestling around them like a whirling veil.

Natasha realized she could sleep with her legs around him, her pussy dripping their sex juices and the far-off electric snarl of music marking the moment.

Sweet God. It hadn't been a fluke. He really was that good. She vaguely wondered at the faint scent of candles that blended in so well with the sex.

Her nipples still tingled and the sensation of her garters cutting into her thighs was a whole new erotic experience.

For this, she'd let him bend her over a pool table.

Or take her—fuck her—in a dark, shadowy corner.

Or . . . sweet Christ . . . she'd let him do damn near anything he wanted.

Garnering up strength, she tugged the blindfold up and looked around at the unexpected sight of candles everywhere—at least two dozen of them—twinkling in the spacious room. If it could be called a room. It was more along the lines of a huge cellar with chandeliers and vaulted ceilings. And quite obviously underground.

Like some dungeon in an opera house. Was he playing the role of beast or madman?

There was a roaring fire in the fireplace not far from where a large bed was turned down. If it were up to her, she'd add a few petals trailing to the bed. It would be downright romantic, she mused.

When she glanced at him, he looked exhausted, annoyed, and a touch defensive. "I didn't order the candles."

Ah. She wasn't sure whether to be amused or insulted. The thought faded as he kissed her again.

Logan's orgasm had been so strong, he'd felt as if a tide had dragged him underwater, the roar of it remaining in his ears. The sound receded gradually, like a spent wave, drawn back to sea. She felt so good in his arms. It felt so incredible to have her hot, sweet body against his, even if his legs were about to buckle. He wanted to lift her again and hold her in the comfort of his bed.

Instead, he took a few strategic steps around and sat on the huge crate by the door, then settled Natasha into his lap.

And that was his biggest mistake, he realized. He shouldn't have brought her into his place when he had no intention of letting her know where he lived. But at this exact moment, she filled his arms so perfectly, it made him realize just how lonely he'd been. His past lovers had been wonderful women, but they'd never wanted to get involved deeper than just the fun and sex. At least this time he knew that was the case from the get-go.

Still, there was a part of him that he seemed unable to control, that yearned for more. It tugged in him now in a helpless ache.

How would she react if she knew he owned the bar? Was she the kind to want to stay with him just to seek out some of his famous clients, or was it easier and simpler for her to think he was just a muscle-head bouncer?

For a second, he held her closer.

Right here, right now, he knew exactly why she was with him. Two simple and very agreeable reasons: his cock, and her suppressed sense of adventure.

He kissed her temple, entranced by the slight angling of her head that invited his lips to move down to her cheek.

"You didn't follow the rules," he said, still brushing his cheek against hers.

"Mmm," she smiled. "You mean playing pool? Shoot, rules are meant to be broken, or in your case, bent a little."

"Not my rules." He nipped her cheek.

"Especially yours." The white of her smile made him want to kiss her again. "Besides, you didn't say I had to hit the billiard balls one by one."

"Next time I'll have no mercy," he warned, caressing the moist valley of her cleavage while the edge of his thumbs brushed the pearls. Her smile turned a little shy, but he continued, squeezing the flesh, then parting the fabric until the straps slid from her shoulders.

He pulled her hands down, and with gentle strength, he held them behind her back.

"What are you doing? Let me go."

"No. You're not the only one who can bend the rules."

"This isn't bending them. It's breaking them." Her struggle was more of a shimmy, and it shifted her torso closer toward him.

Chuckling at her weak defiance, he buried his face between her breasts, his forehead slick as his perspiration blended with hers there. He tasted the saltiness of her clean sweat under his tongue and was rewarded by the telltale catch in her breathing again, by her strong heartbeat, by the softness of her skin.

He needed willpower. Needed more self-control, because, dammit, just resting against each other felt inexplicably good . . . like balm on his soul.

Shit. He mentally shook his head. *I sound like a drunk poet.* Dragging his thoughts away, he caressed her breast.

"You like being blindfolded," he noted, before licking her pert left nipple. "You become a different woman."

Her chin went up a notch. "Don't read too much into it. I'm simply indulging your fantasy, that's all."

"So, you don't enjoy it?" He watched her carefully as he licked his way to her other breast.

She shrugged, careful not to dislodge her breast from his mouth.

"Come on, confess—"

"You know, if you're going to keep talking, I'm going to just play with the vibrator."

He grinned and nipped her skin. "It wasn't a difficult question."

She was just squirming against his semi-erect cock when his cell phone cut into the moment with a shrill.

He reached one hand into his sagging pants to kill the noise. The red blinking light was the mute news flash that there was some trouble going down upstairs, and he was being given a heads up. It was probably the senator's daughters, he realized. It hadn't been the first time they had become belligerent enough to be kicked out of the bar.

His manager could handle it.

He looked up in time to see Natasha's gaze grow cool and calm despite the passion of just seconds ago. She was oddly calm. "Let me guess. You have to go," she said, almost accusingly.

"No."

Her kiss-puffed lips thinned with disapproval and something else. Something that made him want to take another look at her.

Her gaze remained wary, then she glanced away. He could sense her tuning him out, her thoughts unreadable. Her cool retreat was so quick, it was sucking the magic out of the moment.

Dammit, was her mind on another man? She was here with him, and he'd be damned if he was about to let anyone or anything interrupt them.

"Take your clothes off," he said, placing a kiss on each breast, marking each with a little bite. "Everything goes but the nylons."

"What?" Startled by his command, she could only stare at him. That damn shrill of his phone had been a cruel reminder of Eugene.

That exact tone had been the one that Eugene had jumped to, regardless of what was going on. A surgeon's duty, he'd reminded her, was more far more important than finishing up sex. As she discovered later, it had less to do with surgery than his other lover demanding his time.

Logan's tongue flicked over her right nipple, and it instantly puckered. "You heard me. Take it off, nice and slow. Strut over to the bed and show me your long-ass legs."

It took her a moment to realize he was serious. "I don't strut. Or shake my ass for anyone."

He nuzzled her cleavage, inhaling deeply. "Why not?"

"Because . . ." Her thoughts got fuzzy as his mouth searched out her left nipple. "Because . . . um . . ." Hell, he asked as if he had a legitimate right to see her strutting. His mouth was starting to seriously distract her, but she told him, "I need a quick shower first."

"Are you sure? Maybe I can change your mind. God, you have legs that would make any man fall on his knees."

Even if he was lying, part of her was thrilled by his words.

Somehow, he had her almost undressed by the time she registered the cooler air on her skin. By the heat in his kisses, his sex drive sure recovered well. Serious bonus points for that.

"Let the games begin," he murmured.

Damn . . . He was kissing her senseless again, tugging her upward until they were both standing.

Time blended into a whirlwind of sensations, of endless kisses, firm caresses, and quivering orgasms that made her utter things she'd never thought to say.

He wound her hands in velvet ropes, tied them to one of the bed posts, and started between her thighs. She clenched her thighs around his head, the lacy edge of her nylons clamping over his ears as she ground her pussy against his mouth, his wide palms holding her to his mouth like a ripe melon. She squirmed with growing desperation, his braids causing erotic sensations as they rubbed against her skin like fingertip caresses.

She was still lightheaded in the aftermath when he bent her over the bed and slid into her from behind, almost rough and edgy with repressed desire, his weight crushing her against the mattress with each thrust, his heartbeat thundering against her spine. He nipped the roll of her shoulder, the delicate curve of her collarbone, his harsh grunts of release hot against her ear when he finally ejaculated hard and deep inside her.

He was a marathon kisser, she realized. He'd start with a simple kiss, tender and almost poignant, the rough, sensual rub of his braids trailing down to touch her cheek and neck, adding to the sensations. She thirsted for him, for more, getting feverish when he went in for the kill, taking her breath, making her blind with need.

She was reduced to begging twice—or was it three times—when his thick cock was inside her, unmoving, and his thumb was slowly and sweetly rubbing her clit until she cried out to be *goddamn fucked*, her hands twisting the velvet rope in an effort to escape the torture. He cussed, in gravelly whispers that sounded like mumblings, in commands that invited disobedience. All of it fell into a magical spell, all of it fogging up her mind.

"Logan . . . I need you to move inside . . . Ahhh."

"Jesus—Tasha, be still. . . ."

"I n-need—"

"—just fucking be still, or I swear to God . . ."

She disobeyed, squirmed, and was punished: his hands gripped her ass in place as he left a love bite on her earlobe.

"If you want it, take it like I give it to you."

"Logan, damn you, if you don't . . ." She tossed her head, delirious with need, gasping for air.

". . . Too slow?" he asked, thrusting.

"Yes! Oh, God . . . Ahhh."

"That's right, babe. Take it . . . deep like that . . . yesss . . ."

"Oh fuck . . . oh . . . fuck . . . Logan . . ."

He kept the pace hard and slow, his cock honing in to her orgasmic spot like a goddamned missile.

She shifted restlessly, selfishly, greedily riding his thick erection for her own wet orgasm. And yet, he controlled her, his love bites splintering and doubling the pleasure, his abs rolling as he set the pace of each thrust. She cursed him, begged him, and whipped through another orgasm with his name on her lips. . . .

At one point she'd woken up to find her legs spread-eagle, her ankles tied to the bedposts, but her hands freed. She'd tried to reason with him then, too, demanding to be released, only to succumb to the persuasive seduction of his mouth and his tongue licking her, tonguing between the folds of her sex and her ever-sensitive clit.

He didn't treat her vagina like a scientific project, to be inspected and parted, but rather like her own mouth, to be ravaged and nipped and teased until her thighs trembled.

All those condoms had made her vagina hyperaware to even his very breathing. The velvety lick of his inquisitive tongue wrecked her weaknesses until she was arching off the bed, holding handfuls of his braids and shaking in gasps as she came undone.

She hadn't known she could come like that . . . all but screaming and helpless from the strong muscle-spasm, deep in her gut, clenching her teeth to keep from begging . . .

Condom wrappers were littered around the bed, marking the hours, the scent of candles enhancing the indulgence of sex. He seemed possessed, like a man who had been without sex for years and was intent on making up for it.

Much, much later, she woke up alone, spent and exhausted.

She donned a robe she found at the foot of the bed and followed the sounds of running water that drew her to a door she'd failed to notice before. Pausing at the doorway, she took in a spacious bathroom, admiring the two large ceramic lions' heads on the wall as water cascaded from their wide mouths.

Logan was standing by the sink, deliciously naked, seemingly unaware of her admiring his wide back and tight butt while he proceeded to brush his teeth.

Hmm, he had an interesting tattoo over his right shoulder—almost covered up by his braids—of an eagle with one eye reflecting the American flag and the other reflecting . . . a Russian flag? How odd. Why a Russian flag?

Nope, she didn't want to know. Shouldn't even ask.

With a sigh, she realized she'd yet to take that glorious cock of his into her mouth. She swallowed dryly, surprising herself by the strong urge to feel that length against her tongue, nestling against the roof of her mouth. Sliding in and out, that plumlike tip filling with each stroke, his length growing more rigid.

Oh, mmm mmm mmm. What's more, that man needed to feel his velvet ropes tighten his skin for a change. Maybe she'd have him spread-eagle, except she'd bind his hands as well, just to be sure he was helpless, completely at the mercy of her desires. But would that be torture enough? She'd heard things about cock rings, so maybe . . .

Logan's gaze caught hers in the mirror, and she tried to hide her thoughts behind an innocent smile.

She politely cleared her throat. "Got a spare toothbrush?"

He held up a new travel pack, and she walked over to take it from him. A comfortable silence settled between them, and as she brushed her teeth, she tried to finger-comb the frightful mess that was her hair.

She'd barely finished rinsing her mouth when he'd tugged off her robe and pulled her into the half-full tub.

"Logan!"

He only chuckled as the cascade from the lion-faucet above fell over them like a small waterfall. She shivered against him, burrowing into his body heat, her face against his neck, trying to dispel the water that seemed to alternate between hot and cold. They remained that way until the water levels reached the tops of her breasts, and then he turned the flow of water off with a twist of a knob.

The blissfully hot water seeped all the way to her bones. She rubbed her foot lazily against his, peering through the thin steam that hovered over the water and into the bedroom where the remaining candles still twinkled.

His hand lingered over her spine, his voice rumbling and deep beside her cheek. "Can't decide."

"Hmm?"

"I can't decide. Whether I want to take you again, slow and easy, here in the tub . . ."

"Or?" She tipped her face upward, seeing the calm mischief brewing in his eyes.

"Or I could make dessert out of your mouth, your breasts, and work my way down."

She peered at him. "How in the hell do you keep going? Are you on some medication that keeps giving you marathon erections?"

He grinned. "No. I've just been too busy to indulge for a while. Guess I'm making up for lost time." His hands continued to run up and down her back, stirring the water into swirling eddies that caressed ever so gently.

"I think—" The unmistakable shrill of his phone sounded from the bedroom, cutting into the moment like a knife. She couldn't help the stiffening of her spine.

"Ignore it," he advised, seeming to have no problem doing so.

But the hated, familiar ring tone dragged her thoughts into the grimy quagmire of the past . . . back to Eugene reaching for his phone, lying to her about having to work late, lying to her about needing her, loving her.

It dredged up all the jealous arguments, the way his pathetic excuses had continued to strangle her suspicions without killing them . . . but worst of all, it brought back that nasty self-loathing that had reduced her to an insecure, petty, and jealous woman. She hadn't been "enough" for him. She'd wondered if she hadn't been creative enough. Or woman enough. Sexy enough. Or . . .

Fuck.

There were a million ring tones in the world, so why the hell did Logan have to use the same one as Eugene?

"What's going through your head?" Logan asked.

"Nothing."

He tipped her chin up so he could see her eyes. "Bull."

She raised an eyebrow at him, struggling with a visceral anger that was close to breaking the surface. "Bull?"

"Does that bother you?"

She ducked her head. "It's just that ring tone."

"I can change it."

"Don't be silly. It's not important."

"It took the smile off your face."

"So?"

"Let me guess. An ex, or—"

"Logan, drop it. It's *not* important."

He paused. "You're right. Although, sometimes it helps to talk."

She eased away from him, the water shifting quietly to fill the gap, rushing in like her emotions. Still, she kept her voice level, struggling to hold back all that old anger and hurt. "We can't do this. I'm sorry, but you can't go there. That topic is off limits. It's not now, nor will it ever be, up for discussion. We schedule the sex, we enjoy the sex, but the rest is private. Less complications this way."

"Tasha—"

"No."

"But—"

"Look, what's so hard to understand? It's simply none of your business. I don't get to ask you where this sex chamber is, what you do, or who you are. And vice versa. That is what we signed up for, right?"

Shit, shit, shit! Why hadn't Logan left well enough alone?

The concerned look ebbed from Logan's face, replaced by a responding flash of anger that, surprisingly, he kept in check. In a blink, the careful emptiness fell over his face, causing her to cringe inwardly.

"You're right, of course," he said. "I clearly signed up for a fuckfest, and the hell with having any personal discussions. So, hey, why are we even talking. . . . Wanna fuck?"

The last few words fell with the sharpness of an axe blade lodging deep into soft wood. His mocking tone dripped with more than sarcasm.

Without a doubt, the sensuous mood they'd had was now completely blown to smithereens.

"I'll pass. It's getting late. I should go," she said, before getting out of the tub.

She bundled up in a towel and, without a backward glance, went into the bedroom to change. The haunting scent of the candles made her regret her outburst even more.

She heard the water sloshing as he moved out of the tub, but she focused on pulling on her dress, tucking her nylons into her purse, and finding her scattered shoes.

Goddamned ring tone.

She looked under the bed for the missing shoe. She had to get out of here. Find a place to think clearly. Evaluate why she'd overreacted like some prepubescent teenager. It would've been smart to apologize and make light of it. To say "I'm sorry" and follow up with a flip excuse that would ease the tension.

But the words were stuck in her mouth like soft taffy on her teeth.

Where in the hell was her left shoe?

The stint in the tub had soothed some of the overly sensitive parts of her body, but walking reminded her of the erotic ache that lingered in her sex.

From the corner of her eye, she could see Logan walk back into the room, rubbing the towel over his hair and body. He pulled on jeans, a T-shirt, and his trusty jacket.

He gathered the bedcover that had slipped from the foot of the bed and tossed it in a nearby chair. Her lost shoe clattered to the floor, and Logan picked it up and handed it to her.

"Don't forget to put the blindfold on," he instructed.

She frowned down at the limp cloth as she slid on her shoe. Couldn't she just close her eyes and have him lead her out?

"Is this really necessary?"

"It's as you said. You don't have any right to know where this 'sex chamber' is."

Crap, she'd fallen into that one. When she glanced at him, he was too busy putting on his boots to look up at her.

Fine. She tied her damp hair into a French knot, put the blindfold on, and waited.

Moments later, she heard him walking toward her.

Natasha was absolutely right, Logan reminded himself. He shouldn't have probed into the whole ring tone issue. It was obvious as hell that it was a biggie. And whoever the dumb-fuck was that it reminded her of, she'd gone from cool to icy-frost at his question.

So what? So fucking what?

Didn't making love—excuse me, *fucking*!—for several hours entitle him to a question or two? Wasn't there a rule that if someone gives you an orgasm—one that damn near makes you black out—you ought to be able to ask something personal? Was that beyond the scope of the Orchid Soul fuckfest?

And yet part of him wanted it this way. No questions. No nothing. Except sex. It had been their initial goal, right?

Even recognizing his double standard didn't ease his mood. Shit, if she'd asked about his past lovers, he'd probably have answered the same way, more or less. It's just that with every kiss, every intimate touch, he'd felt something more.

So, why was she denying it? Hell, she was here now, blind-folded, trusting him to take her back to her comfortable real-ity. He took a moment to study her pulse racing just below her jaw, to admire her puffed lips, and resisted the urge to kiss her again. Incredibly, his overused penis twitched with the beginnings of arousal.

He reached up silently and had barely touched her cheek when she jerked back in surprise. Suddenly, she whipped her hand out, hefted with her body, and he found himself flipped through the air, landing on his back with a thud that knocked the wind right out of him.

Pinpoint stars danced in his vision, but too many years of fighting had him reacting, grabbing her ankle and tugging her off her feet. She fell toward him, and he had just enough time to suck in a breath, catch her, and roll her onto her back.

They fought as they tumbled, and she managed to straddle him just long enough for him to twist and flip her again.

Her knee came up.

He blocked.

She threw a quick, unexpected shoulder strike that jarred his teeth.

Checking the instinct to strike back, he rolled just enough for her to scramble away. In a flash, she'd pushed up the blindfold and quickly assumed a fighting karate stance.

"What the hell was that about?" he asked. Logan rolled up to his feet, his dumb cock behaving like he'd been promised a blowjob instead of being thrown on his ass. He could hardly look away from her heaving breasts.

"That's *my* question," she all but snapped.

He grinned. "I was just touching you."

"You could've given a warning."

He shrugged, grinned. "Lesson learned. Nice punch, by the way."

"Thanks."

"What the hell did you think I was going to do?"

"Who knows? I just reacted."

He nodded and rubbed his chin. "Are you waiting to toss me around some more? I wouldn't recommend it."

"Don't give me a reason to do it, then." She eased from her stance, narrowing her eyes at him. "But that doesn't mean I can't take you."

"Trust me. I can take you."

She raised a cocky eyebrow. "Huh."

"I'll subdue you, but I won't fight you. I don't fight women. Although if you want to throw in some oil and a wrestling mat, I say bring it. We could start something interesting."

Her sudden smothered burst of laughter had him chuckling.

"Are you always thinking sex?" she finally asked.

"Yup. It's a blessing."

She rolled her eyes at him, but it only amused him more. The tension ebbed for a moment as they eyed each other, and a world of questions he had no right to ask filled him. If he held her down, would she admit to what had ticked her off? Had it been anger talking, or was the none-of-your-business rule a permanent thing? But he sensed there had been some hurt feelings daggered in that reaction of anger—the knowledge cooled his own temper quite a bit. What was up with the fucking ring tone?

She'd made it clear he had no right to know.

Something must've shown on his face because she suddenly gave him a stiff bow, in the traditional courtesy of martial arts. Or maybe it was a truce. Of acknowledgment that a line was clearly drawn between them.

The smooth ease of her move had pointed to long-term study of martial arts, and he'd been a bouncer enough years—more than he could count—to know from the look on her face that she really thought she could take him. Experience, however, had taught him that the finesse of artistic fighting was often lost in the edginess of less elegant, grappling, dirty street fighting. The element of surprise was the key, and she'd had that. But he still could've held her down, helpless, if he'd wanted to.

What did she look like when she practiced the poses and forms? The thought of watching her doing the rigorous, disciplined moves was an unexpected turn-on. Maybe he'd even volunteer to be tossed on the mat again, as long as she covered him with her body again and took full sexual advantage.

And so the fantasies line up, he thought with a sigh.

Natasha straightened her dress, but her gaze cooled a bit, and he sensed she was waiting for him to start asking questions, to cross that fine line that kept them strangers.

Instead he pointed at the blindfold and said. "Come on. We have to get going."

Natasha had followed him out, blindfolded, her hand clasped in his, the feeling so sensitive that she could've sworn she felt each groove of his fingerprints.

She'd expected the trip back to be as long as the one to the chamber, but the long hallways and twisted stairs came and went in no time.

When he finally stopped, she knew they were at the final door, since the music thumping from the other side was so much louder.

"I'm going to take the blindfold off," he murmured, "but first, I have a few instructions for tomorrow."

She frowned. "I told you, I don't do instructions."

"Yeah, yeah." His hands molded over her hips. "Wear the Clit Clip to work."

Oh, *hell* no! But before she could say so, he was kissing her softly, being just a touch demanding, as if he could break her will.

"Did I mention it works like a pager?" His mouth brushed her cheek.

She panted, and tried to focus on what he was saying, but he was subtly grinding his just-stiffening erection against her.

"I figure the battery should last through ten calls."

She swallowed, feeling the tug of response in her gut. "No."

"Oh, yes." And when he kissed her again, she wanted to wrap her legs around his hips for one of his not-so-fast quickies. "I'll start after eight thirty, just to be sure you don't wreck in traffic while having an orgasm."

Considerate, sexy bastard! "You're assuming a lot."

He nibbled her earlobe, the warmth of his breath starting a shiver that snaked right to her nipples. "I promise not to call you twice in a row. . . . Aw, hell, I lied. I just might do that."

She turned her head to tangle her tongue with his one more time. "Not going to do it," she finally managed.

"Mmm-hmm. You will."

She nipped his chin. "Not."

He laid an open-mouth suck just under her jaw. "And Tasha, since I had a wet dream about you, I think you ought to dream about me."

Ah, well, damn . . .

Before she could clear her head completely, he undid the blindfold and opened the door separating her from reality.

Without a word, he led her out, through the shoulder-to-shoulder crowd that seemed to occupy every inch of space to the front door.

She didn't object when he walked her right out of the noise and into the quieter stillness of the night, walking next to her until she reached her car.

He seemed as reluctant to breach the comfortable silence as she. So, she settled into the car and turned the key, noticing that somehow, he'd found a swizzle stick to chomp down on.

Lord knew she could've used a cigarette herself, if only to savor the satisfaction of a fine night of sex.

"Drive carefully."

She was tempted to leave a kiss over the zipper covering his semi-erection.

Instead, she nodded her good-bye.

He winked at her as she drove off.

Natasha half woke from her sleep, dreaming of the tiny humming vibrator while she reached out to run her hands over Logan's shoulders, pulling the man in for a long, slow-hauling thrust.

She tried to kiss him but instead found her mouth filled with the taste of her pillow and the embarrassing reality that she was pushing herself against her mattress instead of Logan's solid body.

All the memories from the night before came crashing down, but then, like morning mist, they began to fade as she drowsed, except for the insistent humming sound. What the hell?

She peered through her narrowed eyelids and found her cell phone twitching in silent-vibrate mode. The alarm clock next to it beamed its neon blue numbers at her, announcing that it was almost seven in the morning.

Dammit, she had to get ready for work. After a couple of blind swipes to the phone, it finally toppled off the dresser and landed on her carpet, the vibrations becoming thankfully quiet.

Feeling deprived of her juicy dream, Natasha closed her eyes and tried to return to the moment Logan had ravished her, his hands like traps, holding her steady for his lavish, amazing kisses . . .

"Damn." She pulled the blankets over her head.

With a huff and a groan, she reached over the bedside and groped for the phone until she found it, blinking to focus her eyes.

An Orchid Soul message popped on the screen.

> Your ff +#following fantasy has been forwarded to your
> I # & = candidate:
> th~ her :"@ #!@@3!—fk#^"tonight. Thank you.

It took a few seconds before understanding settled in.

Orchid Soul had finally lost it. Natasha groaned and chuckled. What was up with that system? And where was Eileen, for crissakes?

She rubbed her eyes, then tried calling Eileen again. This time, when the call bounced to voice mail, the message said the mailbox was full and advised her to try back later.

The niggling worry about her friend grew stronger. Why

hadn't Eileen called her back? Even as she stared at the phone in thought, it rang again. Maybe, by some miracle, it would be Eileen. She answered it.

"Hello?"

"Sure picked that up quick," came Logan's deep drawl. "I take it you got the e-mail?"

"What e-mail? The one that's nothing but garbage?"

He paused. "Garbage? Hmm." There was another pause. "I didn't get garbage."

She shook her head to clear it. "What did you get?"

He exhaled, and she wondered if he was exhaling smoke. Man, what she wouldn't give for just one puff. . . . "I got a double-oh-seven fantasy."

What? "As in James Bond?"

"Yup."

"That's strange. I sure didn't submit one."

"Really?"

"Yup."

There was a short pause. "Huh."

They both paused as the implication sank in. If Orchid Soul was sending wrong fantasies to them, it stood to reason that it was also sending their fantasies to others. No anonymity and now, no privacy either?

"So, um, what's it say?"

"Let's see," he sighed, sounding deliciously groggy. "Basically, it's about a secret agent who captures the enemy and tries to make him talk by any sexual means necessary. Not bad."

"What do you mean? It's not ours. We can't just use someone else's fantasy."

"Why not?"

"Because . . ." It just seemed wrong.

He seemed to be waiting for a better argument, but her groggy mind couldn't come up with one.

"You'd make a hot Bond girl."

"Oh yeah. Bet your ass I would," she mumbled, mocking herself.

He made a purring sound that vibrated against her ear. "And you can call me Dr. Yes."

She closed her eyes and tried not to laugh. "You've given this some thought."

"I have. I'll e-mail you the info."

"It's not right."

She could hear him moving and imagined the bedsheets sliding down his body. "You're not thinking straight. Have some coffee, read my e-mail and get back to me. And by the way, don't forget to set your tiny toy to pager mode when you get to work."

Oh, hell. "I told you I wasn't going to do that."

"Yeah, I heard. You may want to take a spare change of undies, too."

"What part of *no* don't you underst—"

"I gotta remember not to call you before you've had your coffee."

He was chuckling as he hung up.

She stared up at the ceiling.

No way was she going to show up to work with a Clit Clip humming away in her thong. It was crazy! Normal people didn't do things like that.

Of course not.

Nope.

Doing this was clearly crossing from fantasy over to reality.

Ten minutes later, she was standing under the shower, washing away the last dregs of sleep and wondering why she was still considering it.

"That's just stupid," she grumbled to herself, her movements slowing as an idea bloomed.

He didn't need to know!

She could wear the Clit Clip and lie to him about it later. No harm, no foul.

Logan's spy fantasy was in her in-box when she stepped out of the shower, and it was much like he'd described. What had her chuckling was that the villain's name wasn't Dr. Yes, but rather Harden McCock.

"Oh, Jeez."

Her reply was brief, letting him know she'd schedule a time, place. Why not? On a whim, she added, "This is not your mama's James Bond. Bring assless chaps."

She contemplated it for a moment, finger hovering over the button to send the e-mail. Would he dare? She took a breath and pressed the button.

And that, she decided—when she finally got around to her steaming cup of coffee—was going to be totally worth it.

Natasha had just made it past the lobby and into the elevator when she noticed her parents hurrying to join her, calling out to her to hold the elevator.

As they all stepped inside, her mother, Benita, brushed her perfect bangs from her forehead while beside her, Natasha's father, Caleb, smoothed his tie. "Good morning, dear. Nice day today, isn't it?" he asked.

The ever-present tension hummed between them.

"Good morning to you, too. Yes, it is."

"You're looking pretty today," her mother commented.

Natasha resisted the urge to check her hair, her lipstick, her clothes. "Thanks. You, too."

But Natasha waited for more.

Her mother wasn't prone to making small talk in elevators without a reason. As always, her parents were dressed like the legal sharks they were, both commanding attention with their lean good looks. Benita had been an attorney for as long as Natasha could remember. Her father had practically been born in a three-piece suit.

Growing up under their shadow, it went without saying that Natasha was expected to follow in the family business. But Benita never left anything without saying.

Most days, Natasha honestly felt she was a good lawyer but never as good as some others in the firm, which, she sensed, was a bitter disappointment to her parents. Well, to her mother. The truth was, law just didn't fire her up the way it did her parents.

"So, tomorrow is my baby's birthday, huh?" her father said with a smile. "Twenty-six years old."

"Think you can squeeze in a lunch with us to celebrate?" her mother asked.

"Lunch?" *To sit through a tense meal together? No way.* But the unexpected tender look in her mother's eyes caught her off guard.

"You know, it's that meal between breakfast and dinner?" her father put in.

Natasha couldn't think of the last time she'd had a casual lunch with either of them. It was always a power lunch with a client or a briefing lunch. Or the single-life thing.

Something was up. She hoped to God it wasn't another "Let's talk about Eugene" chat. Things were strained enough with her mother as it was.

"Ah, Mom, I actually had plans," she lied.

"Oh." Twin eyebrows went up with a mixture of suspicion and disappointment. "Well, maybe day after tomorrow? Or . . . soon?"

"Sure." In legalese, soon meant anything from next week to forever, didn't it?

As the elevator chugged upward, Benita reached into her purse and pulled out a box already wrapped with a bow on top. Natasha mentally winced.

The familiar jeweler's name on the box gave it away before Natasha had even opened it. But she did so anyway.

"A pearl necklace. How . . . lovely!" She hoped it sounded sincere, but she couldn't help wondering if her mother kept a stock of jewelry boxes in a drawer someplace the way most people kept boxes of pens.

Natasha gave them both a brief hug, hoping she was the only one sensing the awkwardness. "Thank you. You really shouldn't have."

Her mother waved it off. "Let's see what it looks like," her mother coaxed. "I got it a little longer this time."

Natasha was about to protest that she was already wearing a necklace, but realized she wasn't. Trying to hide her reluctance, she took the perfect string of white pearls from their jeweled cushion and put the necklace on. They weighed heavily on her neck.

"They are lovely. You wear it well," her mother said, echoing the exact words Logan had once said to her. Except—holy cow!—was there a sheen of tears in her mother's eyes?

"Our little girl is all grown up." Her father uncharacteristically put his arm around his wife's shoulders in a show of affection and, somehow, protectiveness.

Natasha wasn't sure what to say. "Mom?" she asked, hearing the worry and confusion in her voice.

"Yes?" But Benita had her composure back, making Natasha wonder if she'd imagined the whole thing.

Since the elevator doors were already opening to the sleek lobby of Madison and Madison, Attorneys at Law, Natasha smiled, feeling more genuine as she said, "Thanks."

Natasha was heading toward her office, mulling over the events in the elevator, when the first page from Logan began to hum like a hungry, wet kiss between her thighs.

Benita felt her husband discreetly squeeze her hand as they exited the elevators. Natasha moved clumsily and her briefcase fell, spilling some documents, which she quickly bent to gather. When Natasha looked up, she looked flustered and embarrassed.

Benita almost went to help but sensed she'd only be shooed away. It was par for the course these days.

Disappointment tugged at her heart, but Benita turned and went into her office, her husband following close behind. It was her fault, really. She hadn't known how to be . . . maternal. It was so much easier to be the professional.

"Honey." Her husband's endearment was followed by a quick massage of her shoulders. "You should tell her. Today."

"Tell her how?" she replied without turning around. "In the middle of lunch? Something like, 'The weatherman says it's supposed to rain today. Oh, and by the way, I've been diagnosed with a cyst in my ovaries. It was caught in the early stages, but, hey, I figured you'd want to know.'"

"Ahhh, honey." His murmured words were choked, the pain there raw enough that she couldn't turn to look at him. Her man. Her king. Her everything.

She stared blindly out the window.

"Sorry." She so rarely apologized, it felt insufficient. Hell, she rarely did anything at the cost of her pride.

For a moment they stood together, him behind her. Then he placed a kiss on her cheek. "My schedule is open for lunch."

She swallowed past the lump of emotion clogging her throat. "How about some Thai?"

"You buying?"

"You bet."

"I'm there." This time she did turn, cupped his face in her hands and gave him a brief kiss. "Why do you put up with me?"

"I adore your Pollyanna outlook on life." His eyes twinkled.

She laughed, as she knew was probably his intent. "You're nuts. Now, scram. I have loads of work to do."

He kissed her back but stayed where he was. "I love you."

"There you go, getting all mushy again," she teased, as she wiped the trace of lipstick from his lips with her thumb. Did he have any idea how much she loved him? Why couldn't she, even now, say those words to him as easily as he did to her? She'd shared an office next to his for countless years. She'd shared her bed, body, and soul even longer. And she'd never been so afraid to lose him.

He'd been her rock, her constant touchstone. It hadn't seemed necessary to state the obvious.

"Take it easy today, okay?" He touched her cheek. "I'll swing by to pick you up for lunch."

He had just turned to leave when she said, "Love you, too."

He paused in the doorway, his eyes worried even though he smiled. Her heart tugged when he seemed to force himself to walk next door to his office.

Five ❧

Having punched in the numbers to Natasha's Clit Clip, Logan stood in the parking lot, taking a moment to wonder about her reaction. He grinned, knowing Natasha would deny ten ways to Sunday that she'd even worn the thing. He could almost imagine her innocent expression when he'd ask her about it.

His heart was doing that yearning thing again, he realized. Just the thought of her kept the ever-present loneliness at bay.

Pulling out his car keys, he unlocked his car and settled in, his mind reigning his thoughts to his trip out of town.

Lots to do today.

His childhood friend, Ivan, was getting out of prison, and Logan was going to be outside when the gates opened and the man walked free. Ivan had done time for driving drunk—an act that took the life of a mother and child. It had devastated everyone, especially Ivan. The guy had gone from having a promising career in football to doing twelve years.

As far as Logan was concerned, the bond was unbreakable. Hell, Ivan's parents had all but adopted him.

Now, years later, Ivan needed a fresh start, and there was no question in Logan's mind that he was the one to help.

What would Natasha think? He sighed. What did it matter? Things weren't supposed to get that personal, anyway. Trying to ignore the part of him that gave that inexplicable yearning tug, Logan reached for his phone and pressed redial.

Six ❧

Natasha fumbled the desk phone she'd been about to use and crossed her legs to savor the delicious tremor that had just started between her legs. Oh . . . man . . .

The whole wear-the-vibrator-to-work idea was a *big* mistake. She couldn't concentrate on work. Couldn't even walk normally down the halls.

And she was going to switch to the fresh undies *soon*.

Already she'd been asked whether she was feeling well when she'd leaned against the table in the break room and hadn't been able to hold back a tiny moan at the unexpected jolt of the vibrator.

Someone had even suggested that she might be catching a stomach flu and should start on some flu medication.

Could they not see that she was blushing and perspiring from lust? She felt as if her nipples were poking right through her jacket. So this was what it was like to feel sex-drugged and aroused.

Oh, daaaamn!

The need to be penetrated was hot and hungry inside her. Her skin itched to be touched. She found herself thinking of the freedom of the blindfold. Of finding a secluded spot to take matters into her own hands.

Lord, if Logan had been anywhere within sight, she'd have jumped and humped him before he got a word in.

Argh! She squeezed her thighs together, capturing the last of the quivers that had her breathing with her mouth open. Fuck, she needed to *fuck*!

But there was work to do, folders to be reviewed and a stack of papers teetering in her in-box awaiting her signature. Not to mention a possible afternoon meeting with a client and a make-believe lunch she'd lied to her mother about.

Right now, though, all she needed was a few seconds to recover, to gather her composure before heading for the restroom to remove the torturous device before facing the workload.

A timid knock on her door had Natasha looking up to find her mother peering in.

"Natasha, if you're not doing well, just go home."

Crap! She sat up straight. "No! I'm fine."

"You don't look fine. You look a bit under the weather. Go home, take some meds and a nap. It will work wonders."

"No, seriously. I can—"

Her mother gave her a look she reserved for the courtroom. "Never take your health lightly. As a matter of fact, I insist you go home right now. You look flushed. Are you running a fever?"

"Um, no. Really, I can't do that. I have a client—"

"I'll have it rescheduled."

When exactly had Benita become this maternal? Natasha felt like a child when her mother walked up to her and placed a hand on her forehead.

"You *are* a little warm," Benita mumbled with a frown.

"I-I, um—"

"Go home. That's an order."

An order? Seeing the stubborn look on her mother's face, she conceded. "Okay. I'll go home. But I—"

"No buts. You're flushed and feverish. Could it be that you caught the flu that's going around?"

"Um, yeah."

"See? Go home and take care of yourself. I'll check in on you tonight." With a stern look, her mother left.

"And this is how people end up in hell," Natasha muttered to herself.

Ten minutes later, she had removed the tempting Clit Clip from her undies and rushed out of the building, feeling as if everyone was hanging out the windows, shock on their faces as they watched her leave.

Instead of going home, Natasha hit the karate dojo, showering before she joined the others on the mat. The discipline of kicks, punches, and rolls helped clear her mind.

By the end of the session, she was completely sweaty and worked over, but she felt calmer, more objective.

She'd just entered her home when Vanessa called. "Hey, what're you up to?"

"Just got back from the dojo. What's up?"

"I'm guessing the same that's up with you," Vanessa said with a sneaky chuckle.

"What are you talking about?"

"Oh, I already know I'm not the only one getting the real deal out of this Orchid Soul thing. Rusty called me all ticked off when her info was given out."

Natasha wandered into her kitchen and reached into the fridge for a bottled water. "Oh? Who'd she get?"

"I'll tell you if you tell me who you got."

"Oh, hell no." Natasha guzzled water.

"Girl, come on!"

"You first."

Vanessa harrumphed. "It's no one you know."

"Ditto." She stopped halfway to her next sip. "You have any idea who Rusty's man is?"

"Of course, I do."

Natasha laughed. "No, you don't. You ain't that slick."

Vanessa laughed as well. "If my guess is right, Rusty is not even looking for a man. She's probably just lying to us to keep us off her back."

Natasha leaned her elbows on the counter, asking ever so innocently, "So, what's your story?"

There was a brief conspiratorial pause. "I'm sampling."

Natasha stalled by wiping her lips. "I'm . . . sampling, too. You know. Just sampling."

"I'm so glad to know, my freaky friend."

"I didn't say all that."

"Right. Anyway, I was worried there for a minute that Eugene was it."

"Hell, no! He's old news. So, how much are you sampling?"

"Just yesterday I damn near put my back out, and I don't mean gardening."

Natasha almost choked on her water. "And you call me the freak."

Her friend laughed. "I don't know about you, but first chance I get, I'm giving Eileen a big old hug. Speaking of which, have you heard from that girl? She's not even answering my e-mails."

"Mine either. I'm starting to get worried," Natasha admitted.

"Rusty said Eileen was going on vacation, doing her nature hikes and such, so maybe she's just ignoring technology."

"Maybe. I hope so."

"Me, too."

But long after Natasha had hung up with her friend, the sobering thought remained that something might've happened to Eileen.

If no one heard from Eileen in the next couple of days, Natasha knew she'd have to do something about it.

Assless chaps? Seriously? Logan scowled, remembering the e-mail, the swizzle stick clenched between his teeth. Hell, no! How did a man maintain his dignity wearing something like that?

He ran a hand over his hair. Natasha wanted him in assless chaps, so . . .

No way.

Hell, he ought to comply.

Logan handed the clerk at Naughty Devil a large bill as he paid for his new purchases. The woman had been encouraging and, with little prodding, had not only showed him what he requested but helped him select several other things as well. Gold arm bands, for example. And the skimpy black-satin jockstrap that Velcro-ripped right off a body. At that point, why not add a new, high-tech cock ring into the basket? So, in it went.

For your self-control and her ultimate pleasure, the clerk had said.

He'd firmly drawn the line at getting Tasha a strap-on—politely letting the sales clerk know he didn't swing that way.

In record time, he'd gone back to his place, showered, groomed, and donned the garments he'd bought. He chose to wear his trench coat again, unless he wanted to have his ass hanging out for the world to see as he rode down the freeway. There was no way he was going to ride his motorcycle in that getup, so he took his precious midnight-blue 1967 Corvette.

He was looking forward to seeing her in a beehive and go-go boots outfit. Or maybe she'd do a skimpy, clingy number.

It didn't really matter, as long as she was caught up in it. He grinned. She might think she was extracting a phony secret from him, but the truth was, he'd made the whole e-mail up. Hell, the damned Orchid Soul messages were showing up scrambled and unreadable, so where was the harm?

She'd enjoyed the blindfold, so now, he was going to see how much she liked being in control. Seeing as how he got to wear assless chaps, it seemed like a fair trade.

Ass. Less. Chaps.

Hell, before the night was over, he was going to make sure she tried them on for him. Imagining her in only chaps and a smile had his cock twitching with anticipation.

Sweet Lord, he wanted her.

Seven ❧

Logan shifted the grocery bag in his hands and waited for the elevator doors to open. Natasha had booked one of the topmost suites of the elite hotel, which was a shame, really, because he doubted they'd have time to enjoy the view.

Once he exited the elevator, he found the room and, after a quick wardrobe check, knocked on the door.

"Who is it?" There was something odd about her voice.

"Special delivery for Tasha Hussy," he replied. Being a fake delivery man always seemed to work in spy movies. Okay, mostly porn movies.

The door was opened just enough for him to hear the theme James Bond music in the background. He grinned just as he got a glimpse of her face. Gorgeous! She was naturally beautiful, but now she'd done the makeup and hair with some Charlie's Angel–Bond Girl flair. And she was wearing a kick-ass little red dress that was more like a body-length corset—with ribbons all the way down the front, stopping just a breath below her crotch.

It was enough to make him drool.

Her voice was husky and sultry as she said, "Pleaze, place ze delivery on ze table." It was said in the worst German accent he'd ever heard, and yet was so unmistakably erotic.

He stepped inside and heard the door close behind him. The minute he'd set the grocery bag down, he felt her push something against his side. "Handz in the air. Move carefully, Mr. McCock. One wrong move and I'll rip your heart out with this device."

Oh, the accent was so adorable! He turned around slowly, looked down, and realized she was holding something that looked a lot like a TV remote control.

"I don't know what you're talking about. I am only a delivery—"

"Lies!" The control was pushed a little harder into his ribs. "You will do well to tell me where za secret nuclear power plant is."

"Darling," he murmured, "I'm pretty sure Bond had a Scottish accent, not a German one."

She rolled her eyes. "You speak nonzenze! Now, give me answers, Mr. McCock."

"The name's Harden," he said with a mock sneer. "And it's also what I do when I'm around you."

Her lips twitched but she sneered back. "So, you think it iz a game?" She stepped back. "Strip! Nice and easy, now. Show me ze power weapon."

He did, moving as if he had a cactus lining his coat, giving her a chance to see that he hadn't bothered wearing a shirt and that the silk underwear and the special-ordered chaps and boots were pretty much all he was wearing. Except for the golden arm bands the store clerk had insisted on. And right now, they made him feel like a futuristic slave more than a government agent.

Her eyes widened and she looked downright surprised. He took advantage of it to grip her hands, pull them behind her back and take her mouth in a kiss that should've started at the door.

He almost groaned.

It was like coming home. Like a long-awaited, quenching drink. Like magic.

Natasha pushed up against him, shifting her hips and grinding just enough for his cock to want to get out from under its satin confines.

"Tasha," he murmured.

"Shh."

He released her and was about to kiss her again when she pressed the damn cold control against his side, her voice unsteady, her accent shot to hell. "It's Jacqueline. But you can call me Jackie Bond."

Oh, yes. He was enjoying this way too much. "Jackie."

"Harden."

For a moment they grinned foolishly at each other at the pathetic name.

"Is that a command?" he asked.

"Always." She glowered, doing her best to hide her amusement. "How's this for another command. Place your hands in those electromagnetic restraints. I assure you, there is no escaping from them."

She pointed to one of the bedposts by the foot of the bed where she'd cleverly tied velvet rope hoops that had been secured to the overhead support.

Another poke from the control had him walking to the bed. He slid his hands in—the loose knots sagged at his wrists—and stood with his back against the smooth wood.

"You can torture me all you want, Jackie, but you won't get anything out of me," he said, wishing he'd worn an eye patch or something with dramatic effect.

She licked her lips, her cleavage heaving, and announced, "Ve vil zee about zat!"

Natasha reveled in rubbing her hands together, showing off her best evil grin, and spouting off about how she was about to dominate the world.

Walking past his shoulder, she murmured in his ear, "You should consider confessing ze truze, Mr. McCockle—"

"It's McCock."

"Silence! You should not vish to anger me." She pushed away and paced in front of him, watching him, empowered by how he watched her with such blatant desire.

The wide gold bands on his biceps showed off the restrained strength of his muscles. And his firm, wide chest was mouthwatering, but really, there was no looking away from his cock that was already straining the black satin by several tight inches.

She took a slow stroll over to him, letting her fingers trail over his chest. She scraped her nails lightly over his flesh, enjoying the quiet hiss of his breath as she left light marks on his skin.

She'd never done such a thing before, but then she'd never felt like she could. And, yes, she could certainly get used to it. Seeing his reaction was just as thrilling.

She moved closer, running her hands over his, inching closer until her body brushed against him, her overexposed cleavage warming against his skin, her nipples instantly reacting. The texture of his braided hair was sensuous against her brow. A stillness came over him, and his breathing became even more ragged. She laid a soft kiss in the center of his chest, her hand trailing down to his hips, then to his belly, feeling the clench of abdominal muscles at his sharp intake of breath.

Good, she thought, then sank her teeth softly against his shoulder.

"Legs apart," she murmured.

"No."

She gave him a vampire snarl, nipped his shoulder again, and gently tugged on a handful of braids, tilting his head back just enough to expose his strong muscular throat. "Obey me."

"Never." But the gleam in his eyes and the single, quietly spoken word sounded like "Forever."

Keeping her gaze on him, she slid her hand down the length of his satin-covered penis, then cupped his balls, filling her hand with them before giving a gentle, not-so-subtle squeeze.

He flinched, his hands twitching against the velvet ropes, but his stance widened. "You'll pay for that."

"Will I?"

"In kisses."

Man, she could suck his lips right off his sexy mouth.

"Dearest enemy, should I continue the torture, or are you going to talk?"

His biceps flexed as his fingers reclasped the velvet ropes above his head, and the scent of him wafted at her in a mixture of deodorant and hot maleness. "I don't know where the secret hideaway is, I don't know who is hiding the nukes, and I certainly don't know any important secrets. Nothing you can do will make me talk."

"Oh, Mr. Harden . . ." She slowly licked his cheek while gently roll-caressing her palm over his testicles in their satin cage. "Looks like I must take more stringent measures."

His nostrils flared. "Ohhh, by all means. Bring it."

With only inches separating their faces, she stroked him, watching every slight reaction on his face when her fingernails trailed up over his full erection with just enough pressure to be shy of a caress, before she stroked back downward.

His smile faded, leaving only arousal. She cupped his balls again, stroked upward to the bulbous tip of his cock, then choked up on it ever so gently before repeating the process again . . . and again.

Sheer weakness had her leaning forward, her lips almost touching his, before she drew back. "Move into it."

He didn't.

She nipped his shoulder.

With a flex of his hips, his cock thrust into the grip of her hand, the satin barely holding in the rigid length.

"Again," she whispered.

He did, his thrust going deeper, the look in his eyes telling her he was imagining something other than her hand sheathing his cock.

She licked her lips so he could watch. "Do it."

This time, when she stroked downward, the ripping grip of the Velcro tore like fireworks amid the notes of soft spy music. When she stroked back up again, the satin fell away, leaving only his heated flesh in her hand.

He groaned, his breath unsteady as he exhaled.

"Are you ready to talk?" Damn, she forgot her accent.

His answer was to strain forward and leave a tongue-flicked kiss on her lips. "Do what you have to."

"I will," she said, briefly kissing him back, leaving her own lick on his lips, her tongue tangling with his for a fraction of a second.

He twitched in her palm, but she kept watching his face closely, selfishly enjoying the telltale muscle twitch at his jaw that told her his control was slipping.

The realization hit that he was her biggest secret. That she'd never been this brave before, this focused or aroused. She wanted to seduce him, to reduce him to begging her as she'd begged him in the past.

Yes, she decided. She wanted to hear him beg.

With a final stroke, she released his erection and began to undo the first few bows covering her breasts. The deep cleavage almost made her breasts fall out, but the excellent tailoring had the fabric clinging on, just below her nipples.

The fact that he looked mesmerized by the sight had her undoing the bottom three ribbons, stopping right above her well-trimmed mons, where the flosslike thong was barely keeping her wetness from dripping down her thighs.

He groaned. "Okay, I'll tell you what you want to know, but you've got to let me taste you a little. Fuck that, make that a lot."

She got in his face, her breasts brushing against his chest. "You don't call the shots, Harden McCock. I do."

For what felt like an eternity, he stared at her breasts like a starved man, watched the movement of her lips as she licked them, then leaned toward her, again, just short of kissing her.

"I'm going to get away, and when I do, I'm going to bend you over the couch and—"

"And what, Mr. McCock? You are in no position to make threats."

For a moment, she worried that he'd tear off the rope and charge her. "It's a promise."

Natasha swallowed hard, knowing he would. Praying he would. Melting like hot wax in anticipation of him sliding into her. . . .

"You don't know who you're messing with," she managed, then ignored his mouth in favor of his neck, tasting the strong column of flesh in several butterfly kisses. Widening her stance, she slowly began to descend, licking a path down his chest, over the tight, hard abs, running her hands over the sprinkling of hair that pointed to the prize.

His cock jutted out to meet her by the time her lips hovered over his belly button. The smell of him was intoxicating, clean but slightly musky and undeniably male.

She stopped, her breath warming his cock as it waited before her like some sort of microphone. She'd never thought a man's cock could be the most beautiful thing on earth, but his drew a primitive, base craving from her. It deserved to be stared at, adored, and intimately kissed.

The need to pay homage to it had her flattening her palms against his chaps as she licked the essence of him from the tip of his cock.

Above her, Logan hissed, and the sudden ripple and clench of his thigh muscles registered under her hands. She licked again, curling her tongue under the tip of the head, swirling around again before covering the entire head in a small, soft kiss.

Logan exhaled in a harsh gasp.

Her breasts ached, her pussy wept, but she was determined to devour his luscious cock in ways he'd not soon forget.

"Do you still have nothing to say?" she whispered, nuzzling his erection with her nose, rubbing it against her cheek, then trailing kisses down one side before doing the same to the other side. To keep from immediately touching his balls, she ran her hands up and down his chaps-clad thighs, doing nothing more than leaving licks and occasional nibbles on his straining dick.

"I'll tell you anything, just please . . ."

She rubbed her hands closer to his inner thighs, her kisses involving a bit more suction. That blunt head of his cock was captivating. Dark and taut, like the head of a large forest mushroom. No, more like a helmet on a missile. Dammit, no—she filled her mouth with just the head again—it was like some sort of sinful candy she could lick for days.

"God, Tasha . . . Damn . . ."

As if she had all the time in the world, she caressed his testicles on either side. Yes, a length like that was too much to take at one time, but why not try? She tongued the length of his cock from the base of his testicles to the tip, humming with appreciation as it strained for her.

Above her, he groaned and muttered words she couldn't understand. His cock felt like steel encased in skin, the thick vein snaking over his erection proving to her he was more than ready to come.

As she stroked his balls in her hands, she kissed the head of his cock and kept going, taking as much of him as she could, then curling her tongue around him as she came back up.

"Oh . . . !"

Sucking him once wasn't enough. Closing her eyes, she took him again, memorizing the width of him in her mouth, the depth she kept trying to adjust, the uniqueness of him that stroked so intimately against her tongue. The scent of him filled her nose, the taste of him was darker than any of his kisses. Each stroke denied her the deep plunge she craved in her pussy, yet it aroused her as much as it did him.

Above her, his moans were peppered with profanity. Blindly, she worked him with her mouth, building a rhythm until she could stroke his testicles and suck him at a timed cadence. His hips picked up on the pace, and his groans matched the plunging action.

Unable to stand the empty grip of her vagina, she lowered a hand to where the ribbons teased her sex, finding the wet labia and delving in before stroking back up to her sensitive clit. She moaned with him in her mouth, rubbed her breasts against his chaps and did it all over again.

His cock seemed to swell just a bit more in her mouth, his slightly tart pre-cum signaling how close he was.

Suddenly, she stopped, her heart thundering while she tried to capture her breath as well as her remaining self-control.

She stepped away, hurried to her purse, and returned with a condom, which she slid over his erection, anchoring it in place with a special cock ring intended to keep him from ejaculating.

"*God, Tasha, please!*" His groan was a raw plea that seemed to strain from the very fiber of his being. And yet, he didn't break free, didn't look angry.

His eyes were full of lust—and something more. Unmistakable trust. From that single look he gave her, she knew he would do whatever she said, endure whatever tortures she intended for him. She was well and truly in control.

"Sit on the bed," she ordered urgently.

Since his hands were still tied to the bedpost, he turned toward the corner of the bed and sat, his hands still above his head, his cock jutting out like an ebony cucumber.

Turning her back to him, she began to lower her thong, milking every second as she bent at the waist, pushing her underwear to her ankles.

His groan was arousing and primal.

Turning back to him, she sashayed to the edge of the bed, well aware that the only things keeping the dress on her body were the two ribbons right above her belly button.

Being careful of the high-heeled shoes, she climbed on the bed and eased closer to him until her slippery wet pussy almost touched his cock.

She caught her reflection in the dresser mirror, an image of her mouth parted in yearning, as if she was half-drugged . . . of her breasts tight and spilling from the dress . . . of her rounded ass arching as she slid down on Logan's rigid cock, deliciously thick.

"Aaaaaah . . . !" Her eyes shut, the jagged pleasure so muscle-twitchingly intense it almost bordered on painful.

Her sex welcomed his cock the way her mouth had, but more so, sheathing more of him than she'd been able to handle orally.

Her legs felt tingly and weak, her high heels wobbling where she'd set them on the bed frame. His hips flexed as she hurried to do it again, his cock stroking another deep, juicy thrust, followed by another . . . and another . . . and . . .

"Fuck!" She thought it, but he spoke it.

She quivered deep inside her womb, the tip of his cock stroking closer, sliding toward the G-spot with the spiraling countdown.

"Tasha . . ."

The echo of his voice passed her like a slow bullet. He jacked into her again, dragging another cry of pleasure from her.

Selfishly, she rode him hard, taking at will, thrilling in the power of it and pushing them both to new limits.

Her pleasure crested to dangerous levels just as she remembered to press the tiny button that unclasped the cock ring. As she stroked her clit, he grunted and rolled his hips again, thrusting deeper. The orgasm hit her gut like a hard sneeze, gripping deep inside.

She trembled once again at the feel of his hot cock inside her, the world spinning behind her eyes.

She gripped the bedpost for all she was worth, squeezing against his body, hoping her legs wouldn't fail her as the aftershocks kept rocking inside her.

It seemed as if her heartbeat blended into his, both rolling like thunder, their breaths like gusts of wind.

Much too soon, she was too weak to do more than ease backward on the bed, his cock spent but not exactly soft inside her. She lay there with one hand by her head and the other on her belly, exhaustion threatening to take over.

Her breathing was still unsteady as she said, "You can free yourself now."

With a grunt and a murmured thanks, he lowered his hands from the velvet ropes. He moved over her, and half dragged her with him onto the bed where they lay together.

Using his arm for a pillow, Natasha sighed and slipped into a deep sleep.

Natasha slept weightlessly, floating serenely, like a lily on a lagoon. The dream was veiled in a fine mist as she dreamed of moist, soft kisses that rippled through her like water. She felt she could float forever, but suddenly, cutting into the perfection was a pierced cry, like the warning of a bird of prey. It was muffled, repeating itself until the familiarity began to sink in, and she caught a glimpse of Eugene in the corner of her eye. What the hell was that idiot and his phone doing in her paradise?

"Goddammit, leave me the hell alone, Eugene," she grumbled.

She tossed her head in an attempt to turn away from the noise, but it rang once more before thankfully fading into the silence.

When she finally woke up, it was so early that the sun hadn't even started to touch the curtains of the hotel room.

Her hair hung slightly off the bed, and she noticed the mirror by the dresser, where Logan had had her watch their bodies just an hour before, when they'd engaged in sex again. This time, his fingers had entwined with hers over her clit while the gleam of his condom-covered cock slid in and out of her.

He'd made love to her with her wrists bound by velvet and her nipples being sucked between the criss-crossed ribbons of her dress. Each time she'd rebelled and tried to take over, he whispered the ways he'd promised to take her when she got freed.

And damned if he didn't keep each and every promise.

She'd found that she could be brought to the brink too many times to count and that payback really was a sexy, beautiful thing.

Much later, he'd stripped her naked and pulled her into the hot tub. She'd sat across from him, but he'd found her sensitive feet and massaged them, kissing her ankle.

"It's ticklish!" she protested.

"Would you just stop wiggling?"

"I can't!"

"Mistress," he said, looking not the least bit submissive. "I only wish to pleasure you."

"Of course you do."

"May I?"

He looked so sincere, she nodded.

He washed her feet with sensuous detail, admiring her recent pedicure with too much interest.

"Your toes are adorable," he murmured. Then, to her amazement, he kissed the arch of her foot, the shock of it blasting past ticklish and becoming an incredibly erotic sensation.

The muscles in her thighs twitched with the need to flex her leg, but he continued up to her toes, nibbling on the pads of her foot, then drizzling honey dust on it and suckling her toes, his swirling tongue tracing areas that felt as incredibly sensitive as her clit.

Christ almighty, *that* had been a brand new, beautiful, orgasmic eye-opener! The honey dust had ended up everywhere. And then he'd followed up with some soft gooey nipple candies that had damned near made her speak in tongues.

But now, relaxed as they were, the minor aches left by the passionate sex made themselves known. She wanted to curl into him again, to hold his body heat against hers, to kiss him as if she could keep him. Damn . . . if she wasn't careful, she was going to start getting notions she had no business getting.

Logan's head shifted against a fluffy pillow, his eyes still closed. "Morning."

"Mmm." Yes, it certainly was.

He was still groggy, his voice deliciously deep, garbling his words. "D'you get enough rest?"

She sighed and stretched. "I could sleep ten more hours."

He remained motionless. "Hmm."

She nudged him in the ribs. "How'd you sleep?"

His nose wrinkled as if he had an itch. "I'm lucky if I got twenty minutes. You're insatiable."

She tugged one of his braids. His eyes opened a crack and he grinned, but as the seconds lapsed, she could see the reserve in his eyes, the distancing, the spark between them cooling.

Eugene had looked like that, as if he was hiding something and hoping she would be too blind to see it and question him.

And, well, she had been.

The unease that suddenly swept over her was almost nauseating. So, now that it was morning, he was starting to regret their night of passion?

"What?" she asked.

A light frown marred his forehead. "I didn't say anything."

"You didn't have to. I can see it in your eyes. What is it?"

"What are you talking about?"

She closed her eyes momentarily. He wasn't Eugene. And frankly, whatever was on his mind was his business. Why pry? Still, there was a tiny voice telling her she was the same old fool if she kept her mouth shut.

How many times were her instincts going to warn her that something was wrong before she listened? Up until this moment, she'd felt he was someone different, someone she'd never imagined herself with. Her secret lover. But now he'd woken up with that look in his eyes.

"You can just come out and tell me, you know," she said as she rolled out of bed, grabbing a bedsheet to tuck around herself.

Logan leaned up on an elbow, his braids a masculine mess as they drooped over his face. "I thought you didn't want to get personal about things."

She'd started picking up her clothes, but she stopped, noticing how still he was. "I don't."

He only looked back.

"But what?" she prompted.

He threw the covers back and sat naked at the edge of the bed. "But it makes me wonder what's going through your mind when you say another man's name, after you've spent the night screwing my brains out."

Her breath caught, and her heart iced over for a solid second. From the recesses of her mind, the memory of her dream came to her, the evil chirp of the bird seeming to echo into the moment, becoming the dreaded ring tone of Eugene's phone.

Dammit, she thought she'd moved past this shit!

"It's nothing," she finally said. "It didn't mean anything."

"What didn't?" he asked, tipping his head. "The man's name, or the night of sex?"

"The man. Don't read too much into this, Logan."

A flicker of anger sparked in his eyes as he walked toward her. "I'm not about to be played like that. I'm not about to be another man's substitute."

"Of course you're not. He's ancient history."

"Obviously not."

Her chin went up, and for several seconds, she wanted to tell him everything, but instead she took a deep breath and said, "Some skeletons linger in the closet longer than others, but you can choose to trust me on this. Or not."

"Trust? That's kinda personal, isn't it?"

Yes, it was, dammit. But she suddenly and desperately wanted him to trust her. Wanted him to know how he'd made her night a magical sexcapade, how he'd been the only thing on her mind all night until that damned ring tone had interfered.

But wasn't that saying too much, revealing too much? She needed to think.

"Logan, can we talk about this when I get out of the shower?"

"No."

She tried to step into the bathroom, but it was too late.

Logan whirled her around, cornering her against the wall in a move that tangled her legs up in the bedsheet and left her visibly stunned. He tried to clamp down on the demon within that wanted answers.

"This is ridiculous!" she snapped.

"If you want me to trust you, *talk to me*."

"Let me go, Logan."

"I'm asking for the truth."

"The truth is simple. He's old news. Now, let me go!" Her eyes gave away her attack before she could attempt it. It was second nature for him to deflect it and then hold her wrists behind her back.

The sheets fell down to her waist, baring her warm breasts against his chest. He clung to his anger in an effort to focus.

"If he really meant nothing, you would've explained yourself by now," he pointed out.

She scowled at him, the I-don't-give-a-damn expression in contrast to the vulnerable stubbornness in her eyes.

"Given our relationship, why does it even bother you?" She shrugged, the movement shifting her breast against his chest just enough to make it hard to listen, but then she paused, and he was sure she'd instigated the move to divert the conversation.

"You must not know men very well." Freeing one of her hands, he tipped her face toward his. "Look at me. Take a real, long, hard look."

Wariness clouded the depths of her eyes, but she did so.

He nodded. This was it. Bare aces, as his old man would say. "I'm only going to say this once. Any time you want the truth from me, and I mean nothing but the whole truth, look me in the eye and ask. I won't lie to you."

"Logan—"

"But you'd better be sure it's a truth you're prepared to deal with. You can trust it. You can take even take it to the motherfucking bank. Got that?"

She nodded.

"Yes, I know we have this fuckfest-non-dating arrangement, and I have no problems being your secret lover, but I sure as hell won't be the man you're cheating on your boyfriend with. If you already belong to someone else—"

"I don't!" She was furious now. "I don't belong to anyone, Mr. Taylor. I thought I did once, but it turned out I was wrong. And every time I hear that goddamn fucking ring tone, I get reminded of that all over again. Is that truth enough for you? Shit!"

She turned her head away to glare at the curtains as if demanding that they get the hell out, her shaky breath stirring a strange emotion in his gut.

"I'm sorry."

"No, you're not," she said, turning her angry gaze at him, and for a while, he could almost hear her thoughts turning. She didn't want to cross the line, and they both knew it.

"Hell," he muttered. "Ask me if I've kept a secret from you."

Her eyes narrowed, but she remained quiet.

He sighed. "It's not a big secret, but, since we're confessing . . . I made up the e-mail," he admitted.

To buy a few seconds, he released her hands and braced his against the wall, exposing his torso . . . in the event she wanted to punch him in the ribs.

She frowned, looking puzzled. "What?"

"The Bond fantasy. I made that up. Had I known about the assless chaps, I might've thought up something else."

"The fantasy . . ." Understanding dawned, clearing up the frown on her face and replacing it with confused surprise. "What? Why?"

"Why not? We had a good thing going and Orchid Soul was on the fritz, so I came up with a temporary solution."

She spoke through clenched teeth. "Temporary solution? Who the hell do you think you are? What gives you the right to lie to me?" She pushed hard against his chest with both hands, but he wasn't having it. Any second now, he knew she'd probably throw in a good, hard jab to his ribs and knock his heart right out of kilter, but it was a worthy risk.

"Dammit, Tasha, I'm not going to apologize for making up that e-mail, because when all is said and done, it was just another fantasy in a growing line of fantasies. But that's all there was to it."

She blinked, muttering as if to herself, "Every time I think I know you, I don't. It always starts with little white lies, doesn't it? And I've been such a *fool* about little lies that I hardly saw the big ones. I'm not doing that again. I have Diamond Life values, and there's no room for this in it." She closed her eyes and shook her head. "I think you need to go. I'm through with this game."

When she opened her eyes, he could tell she was as surprised as he was.

They faced off for what felt like an eternity before he stepped back, every instinct telling him not to. "You don't mean that."

She clung to the bedsheet like it was a shield, a great deal of pride in the tilt of her chin. "I certainly do."

He couldn't believe she was making such a stand on one white lie. How had things come to this? Was his lie worse than her talking to Eugene in her sleep? Fuck, he didn't need this headache.

"So be it. It's been fun, Tasha."

His words were absorbed into the stillness of the room before she said, "It's been nice."

Then in a flurry of motion, Natasha stepped into the bathroom and closed the door, shutting him out along with some of the trailing bedsheet.

He wanted to barge in there and somehow make the last ten minutes disappear, but he didn't know how. Lord, he didn't want to leave, but he'd be damned if he would grovel.

He wanted her forgiveness, wanted to erase the memories that haunted her sleep. Hell, he wanted to replace her every dream with raunchy dreams of the two of them.

Well, since he was being honest about it, he was pissed with himself for sabotaging the chance to know her a bit more when she was just being herself instead of this Orchid Soul deviant. He wanted . . .

Shit, he wasn't allowed to want that much. It wasn't like he'd *planned* on wanting that much. But he did.

Logan exhaled a puff of air, then walked back to the bed, shaking his head before changing into his spare clothes. Maybe letting things cool off was the best way to approach this.

He took one final look around, taking one step toward the bathroom door, before he turned around and left the room, wondering why she hadn't punched him instead.

Natasha felt choked up with anger and disappointment. Primarily with herself, for overreacting to the stupid little lie, but why did he have to lie? Why were her lovers always liars?

Ugh, on the flip side, wasn't their Orchid Soul game based

on secrets and lies? And why was she still comparing him to Eugene the loser?

A headache was starting to throb at her temples from all the arguments bouncing in her head. She couldn't shake the image of Logan's face when she'd said it was over.

Natasha stood under the spray of water as it came down like hard, hot rain. She sucked in the steam, exhaling it like cigarette smoke, but it was a pathetic remedy. The silky soap washed away the scents of sex, but the tender spots of being ravished remained. Just as she reached for the knob to turn off the flow of water, she thought she heard a door closing.

Logan had left.

She caught herself staring blindly at the shower door, as if he would reappear. Would he accept an apology? She looked away and rinsed off again. It was silly to feel like she'd just lost more than a lover. Truth be told, she had started to think of him as a friend.

"Dammit, Logan." She gripped the knob, shutting off the water. The steam began to clear, and the coldness settled in.

Fantasies were great. But maybe it was time to get back to reality.

Eight ❧

Natasha had just entered her office and set her briefcase on her desk when her mother walked stiffly into the room.

"Where were you last night? I called twice."

The question was so unlike her mother that Natasha frowned and took a moment to come up with a lie. "I didn't hear anything. I must've slept through it."

"Slept through it?"

"Yes." Natasha busied herself opening her briefcase. "I took some medication for my, ah, fever, and it knocked me right out."

"I see." There was undisguised suspicion in the two words.

"I'm doing much better," Natasha added with a hopeful smile.

"Well, then. That's good." Her mother nodded, as if a judge had just made a fair decision.

Oh, Mom.

"By the way, I have an opening on Wednesday for lunch. Does that suit your schedule?" Benita asked.

Even though Natasha knew the time was available, she flipped through her desk calendar. "Yes, that suits."

"Excellent." After a stiff smile, her mother left, leaving Natasha to wonder what the heck was going on.

For two whole days, Natasha felt grumpy and lonely. She'd stayed a little later at the dojo, working up a hard sweat that had her muscles twitching. It didn't help.

Worse, she walked around like a junkie in need of a fix, and it wasn't just the nicotine urges working her nerves. Those addictive cravings had somehow melded into a persistent, hormonal demand that had her dreaming of Logan at night and during meetings. She tried to get rid of the stairwell recording but instead ended up pleasuring herself to the sounds, reliving each erotic detail, with Logan's name echoing in her head when she came.

She wanted sex! With only Logan. She missed the way he sometimes gave her a look, as if he knew she was craving a smoke, or a kiss, or a laugh. And she loved it when she could figure out what he was thinking.

And thinking about him made her want to chain-smoke a pack of cigarettes. The chalky gum that had helped in the past sure as hell was not cutting it this time.

By the second night, she had worn down the battery of her all-time favorite sex toy, the Clit Clip, and still she felt empty afterward.

The more she tried to push the urges away, the more they persisted. The slightest thing tangled up her thoughts until she found herself staring blankly at paperwork or at a pile of dirty dishes.

She finally jolted out of it when the evening news flashed the breaking story of a mountain rescue of a climber who had fallen and broken her legs. The helicopter cameras were shaky, but the moment it flashed Eileen's face, Natasha jumped out of the couch and stood just feet from the TV set.

". . . was found by hikers, unconscious on the Milo Pass. She has been airlifted to the hospital, where she remains in critical condition . . ."

The phone rang almost instantly, and when Natasha picked up, Vanessa's voice shouted, "Are you watching the news?"

"Yes, yes. Shh, I'm trying to catch it."

She huddled her phone to her neck, but both of them stood silent, shocked as the news continued with the coverage.

"They took her to Saint Mary's," Vanessa said, when they cut to commercials. "Shit, I can't believe it."

"Me, either."

"I've got to go see her."

"Yup, me too. I'll call Rusty, see if she can come."

The drive to the hospital was a blur, and the waiting in the intensive care lobby was Natasha's idea of hell. Vanessa was there when Natasha arrived. Rusty arrived a bit later, looking every bit like the mechanic she was.

Natasha recognized several other friends waiting, but as the night dragged on, the number dwindled.

When it was finally clear that they could see Eileen—for a very short minute—they almost didn't recognize her scratched and bruised face. There were tubes and IVs draped around her like plastic veins. Her legs were in traction and, according to the nurse, she was going to be heavily medicated for a while.

"Is she sleeping?" Vanessa asked, peering at Eileen's half-opened eyes.

"I think so," Rusty said.

"I wish she'd close her eyes," Vanessa whispered. "It's creeping me out."

Natasha hushed them. "Girls, I swear. Behave."

To their surprise, Eileen worked up a ghost of a smile and looked like she was enjoying an inside joke before her smile faded and her eyes shut completely.

None of the monitors beeped in alarm, and they all exhaled shakily.

It wasn't much, that smile, but it was so typical of Eileen that Natasha found herself smiling as well.

"That's Eileen," Vanessa declared, chuckling quietly.

"Thank God," Rusty said, running a hand over her short hair. "She looks so broken, it's hard to tell."

By the time the nurse shooed them away from the room, the worry over their friend had eased a bit.

Rusty shoved her hands deep into her oil-smudged jumpsuit as they headed for the parking lot. "I've been thinking the meanest things about her. Swear to God."

"Ditto," Natasha chimed in.

Vanessa had an arm around her. "Shit, I was starting to think she was in hiding because of all the bugs with Orchid Soul. And all this time . . . I've been getting my freak on."

Rusty and Natasha shared a knowing look, but neither spoke.

Vanessa sucked her teeth with attitude and stopped walking. "Riiiight. Puh-leez, ye who is without guilt hurl the first stone."

Rusty reached down for a pebble, to which Vanessa cracked up laughing. Natasha found herself joining in, along with Rusty. The laughter bubbled, and all the stress of the evening and the days before melted away.

They shared a group hug as good-bye, but still loitered.

"I've got to get back to Twyla," Rusty said. "She's probably driving the babysitter crazy. We're still on for the salon thing this Saturday, right?"

Vanessa brightened. "I'm looking forward to being scrubbed and rubbed and . . . stuff."

Just like that, Natasha's mind reverted to lying in the tub with Logan, his hand rubbing the soft liquid soap up and down her body, from her hip to her chest, his thumb cresting over her nipple, his palm capturing the weight of her breast. . . .

"Sure, I'm in," Vanessa said. "I need a good massage too, swear to God. I might even need the works this time. You know, the whole de-plucked, herbal slather, and apricot-rub thing."

"That sounds like a recipe for chicken," Rusty said with a grimace.

"They certainly treat us like chickens," Natasha noted. "They wrap us up in mud sauce and keep us marinating for about an hour."

"What does that say about us?" Rusty noted. "That we go really well with a fine Napa chardonnay?"

"Speak for yourself. I'm more of a red wine. Something like a merlot," Natasha said. "And Vanessa—"

"I know I go great with vodka."

It was said with such certainty that both Rusty and Natasha laughed.

"And that's all I'm saying, 'cause you both ain't talking about your men, so you don't get to hear more details," Vanessa said, her eyebrows raised.

Rusty reached for her buzzing phone in her pocket. "Oh, would you look at the time. Gotta run. See y'all on Saturday."

"You're such a chicken!" Vanessa complained.

"And you are nosy," Rusty countered with a wide grin. "But okay, all I'll say is that this guy is not . . ." She threw her hands up.

"Not your type?" Natasha asked.

"Yes!"

Natasha shrugged. "Neither is mine."

"Same here," Vanessa admitted. "But he sure can work me. So, what? I want details!"

"You're going to have to wait, sister," Rusty said, chuckling as she headed off.

"Me, too," Natasha said, heading for her car before Vanessa cornered her.

"Y'all best be in a gabby mood," Vanessa called to them. "Because I'll be in full-on Barbara Walters mode."

The following day, Natasha arrived a little before schedule to the bistro, and it was sheer weakness that had her loitering by the public phone booth just around the street corner from the entrance of the restaurant. She was standing just far enough from the group of smokers to be polite and yet close enough to inhale the little smoke that came her way.

To calm her jittery hands, she absently played with the lighter she couldn't make herself part with, mentally running through reinforcement exercises.

No, she didn't need to smoke.

Yes, she could break the habit.

Yes, she was the captain of her own destiny and her health was in her hands.

Calmness, focus, and perseverance would pay off.

"Need a smoke?" One of the men offered her a cigarette, and she reached for it before she could stop herself.

Oh, Jeez. "Thanks."

He offered to light it, but she gestured to the lighter in her hand.

"Waiting on someone?" he asked nonchalantly.

She was dying to put it under her nose and sniff the length of it. Maybe even lick it. "Um, yes, I have a lunch date."

"Oh. Well, then." She noticed his smile was slightly apologetic. "Maybe I'll catch you some other time. Hey, have a nice day."

As he sauntered off, she realized he had been starting to hit on her, but she'd been too distracted by the cigarette cravings to notice.

Sighing, she held the unlit cigarette between her fingers in one hand while flicking the lighter in the other.

The deep-throated throttle of a motorcycle had her scanning the parking lot. Her heart suddenly did a couple of strong hard knocks when she spotted the rider. Even before he took off his helmet, she knew who he was.

Deliberately tearing her gaze away, she leaned against the wall, the visceral need for sweaty, mind-blowing sex—and cigarettes—spilling like a rabid toxin through her veins. Part of her willed him to walk past her to the bistro, yet she sensed him coming directly toward her.

He looked . . . like a nice, long, intoxicating pull of fresh air. His eyes gleamed with a purpose she couldn't define.

"It's not what you think," she blurted, when he finally stood before her.

"You have a fresh cigarette in one hand and a lighter in the other, but you're not planning on smoking it?"

"That's right."

Those eyes of his! God, she missed the way he made her feel. She almost squirmed under his scrutiny.

"This is just a new reaffirmation therapy, Logan. Confronting my weaknesses, you know." She raised the cigarette. "I *don't have to* smoke this cigarette. I can, if that's what I want. But it's about self-control, and not giving in to bad habits, and, um, being smart and responsible for my health. I'm making good choices and—"

Logan made a carnal sound, leaned forward, and slanted his mouth over hers, cutting off her rambling with a long, hard kiss that made her feel as if she'd fallen backward into champagne. There was no time for air, logic, or even thought. There was just the devouring need that ravaged like lightning through her. The velvet seduction of his mouth dragged every spastic, addictive urge from her, releasing the edgy passion that had been eating her up for the last two days.

"Logan . . . God!" She grabbed a handful of his braids in one hand and wrapped the other around his shoulders, pulling herself completely against him until she was almost faint. She sucked in enough air to go under again, sinking fast, losing her grasp on reality and loving it.

His hands banded around her and she felt naked against him, forgetting every reason she'd justified to stay away from him.

"Natasha?" A woman's voice barely cut through the haze.

From somewhere outside the realm of pleasure, the startled words began to register. Against her, Logan stiffened, his erection nestled against her hip, his breath against her cheek. He eased back just enough for Natasha to look toward the voice.

The shocked expression on her mother's face was like a splash of glacially cold water. "Mom?"

"I'll, ah, be inside." Then, slipping her sunglasses on, Benita walked toward the restaurant.

"Oh, shit," Natasha mumbled, burying her face against Logan's chest. He smelled so damned good, so fucking familiar. Her lips felt puffy from the kissing, her breasts felt heavy and achy, and her vagina, honest to God, was soaking wet!

She wanted nothing more than to have him all to herself and block out the rest of the world.

"We shouldn't have done that," she muttered.

"Really?" He nuzzled her cheek, kissed her again, but this time it was a brief, tightly reined kiss with just enough bite to draw out a pathetic whimper from her.

"Did that take the edge off?" His drawl was tinged with breathlessness.

"Was that what you were doing?"

He eased back, putting more space between them, and she

realized she'd crushed the cigarette into his hair and dropped the lighter during their passionate episode.

Lord, she'd lost her mind. Fighting embarrassment, she brushed the tobacco out of his hair, scrambling for normalcy. "Well, thank you for, um, that interesting approach to addiction intervention. It seems to be quite effective."

He too was gathering his composure. The last thing she expected to hear was, "So, you're the daughter of the legendary Benita Madison."

Natasha stopped in mid-motion. "You know her?"

He shrugged, exhaled. "Who doesn't? Both your parents are high profile."

Yes, they were the legal sharks. In comparison, she was the clownfish. And now, she could no longer be his mysterious stranger. The mystique was broken. He now knew who she was—or at least, he had an idea of her place in the real world. She, on the other hand, still had no idea who he really was.

"Well, I'd love to discuss this, but, um, my mother's inside," Natasha said, pointing toward the entrance. "Waiting. So, I should . . ."

"You have to go."

She nodded. *God, she sure as hell would rather be kissing him!*

"I'll call," she said, before she could trap the words. "Or, you can call," she revised.

He half-chuckled.

She squared her shoulders. "Just to talk."

"Of course."

When she couldn't think of anything to say, she walked around him, feeling his gaze on her back. He remained where he was, but if she had to guess, he was probably waiting for his erection to simmer down.

Upon entering the bistro, Natasha went directly to the women's restroom and hurried to undo the sex-starved look on her blushed cheeks and kissed lips. Even a blind man could see the kiss had done nothing to take the edge off.

The thought of facing her mother lodged a cold pit in her gut. Benita was going to be armed for battle. No doubt about that.

"You can do this," she whispered to herself. Hell, she was her parents' daughter, after all. For the next hour, she was going to be a clownfish with big, sharp teeth. Or at least try to be.

With that in mind, she made her way to where her mother was ordering a glass of white wine from the waiter. Wine? During working hours? Maybe it was because Logan looked like a motorcycle gangster.

Natasha straightened, exhaled a shallow breath.

When the waiter left, her mother looked at her as if she was a witness about to be grilled in cross-examination. Feeling challenged by it, Natasha forced a smile.

"Did you enjoy your birthday?" her mother asked.

Natasha shrugged. "It was just another day of the week."

"Did you spend it with your boyfriend?"

Natasha hoped the fresh makeup was hiding some of her blushes. "He's not my boyfriend."

"You don't say. How did you meet?"

"I really don't think it's something I want to discuss."

Her mother's smile widened and Natasha felt her fingertips go cold with dread. "I insist."

Natasha set her poker face firmly in place. "At the risk of insulting you, Mother, it's really none of your business."

Benita crossed her arms and leaned forward against the

table, her eyes like lasers. "Ah, but it is. I don't object to you getting overly amorous in public"—her mother waved her hand as if to say, *making out like a slutty East-Side hooker*—"but, surely you must know that Logan Taylor is a recent client of ours. Two months ago, as a matter of fact."

Natasha couldn't have been more surprised if her mother had grabbed the fork and stabbed her hand with it. She could hardly focus as words like "representing his restaurants," "New York," and "business ventures" came at her like flung pebbles.

The room seemed to spin, rotating around them, dragging the surrounding sounds into the whirl.

"So, do you still think it's none of my business?" Benita asked, then leaned back when the waiter arrived with the glass of wine.

From the corner of her eye, Natasha noticed Logan, and when she caught his glance, he started toward them.

The waiter left just as Logan stepped up, holding his bulky helmet in his hand, not looking one bit like the businessman her mother proclaimed him to be. Without invitation.

"May I join you?" he asked.

"No!" Natasha bit off.

"Yes!" Benita sounded delighted.

He pulled up a chair and joined them.

"Mrs. Madison," he said, calm in the face of Benita's barracuda smile.

"Mr. Taylor, please," Natasha hissed, "This is a private matter."

"Don't be silly," Benita interrupted.

He continued addressing Benita. "Imagine my surprise to find that Tasha Madison is your daughter."

Benita raised an eyebrow at the nickname and looked back and forth between them. Natasha quelled the urge to kick Logan under the table.

Natasha tried again, glaring at him. "Might I have a moment of your time, outside?"

"Are you dating my daughter?" Benita interceded.

"Mom!"

"As a matter of fact, we are dating," Logan said, forcing Natasha to hold her smile like a rabid dog.

"I see." Her mother sipped the wine.

Tired of being ignored, Natasha leaned forward. "Mother, I'm a grown woman. Old enough not to have to explain my dates to you or anyone else, for that matter. I'm sorry if dating Mr. Taylor breaches company policy. It's a situation I intend to remedy soon."

Logan was expressionless. "Is that so?"

"It is."

But the look in his eyes reminded her of the kiss they'd shared a few minutes before. The slight pause in the conversation already said too much.

"Would you be kind enough to leave, Mr. Taylor? I *very much* want to continue this conversation with my mother in private. Please."

He seemed to struggle with the decision, and part of her wondered if he was worried that the firm would dismiss him as a client. After all, business was business.

"All right," he finally said. Reluctantly, he stood, his hand sliding away. "I'll expect your call."

"Expect a call from me as well, Mr. Taylor," Benita said, surprising Natasha.

"I will."

Even though she'd asked him to leave, Natasha felt abandoned when he did.

Benita sipped the wine again, holding the glass next to her lips rather than setting it on the table "Let's overlook the display out front for a minute, and," she took another quick sip, "spare me the line about the two of you dating—"

"Mom, it's my personal business."

"He's a client. What in God's name were you thinking?"

It wasn't as much the tone as the look on her mother's face that had Natasha's stomach in knots. "Obviously, we didn't know. Sorry."

"Sorry? Benita finished her wine. "I don't know what to think. But frankly, it doesn't matter. You will, of course, end this relationship immediately to comply with company policy. Your father and I will discuss the business course of action."

The words were like a final slap, the mask of disappointment firmly on her mother's face. It had worn the same look on the day Natasha had announced that she hadn't passed the bar exam and would have to take it again. And on the day she'd lost her first legal case. It was the absolute wordless statement that Natasha wasn't living up to her mother's standards. Yet. Again.

And that damned look was like a dagger pushing into Natasha's gut each time.

Benita made a disgruntled sound and reached into her purse for lipstick, which she refreshed with aid of her gilded silver compact.

The dismissal suddenly crystallized it for Natasha. She would never win her mother's approval, and, after years of trying, she realized there was nothing she could do to win Benita's praise.

Natasha felt as if her heart was full of pebbles when she

said, "Mom, I've been thinking of leaving the firm for some time. Now seems like a perfect time to give notice."

Benita lowered the compact mirror in degrees, her face only slightly pale, her eyes wide with surprise.

"Dear, I don't think—"

"I'm sorry. My decision is final." Natasha rushed the words out before they died on her lips. In her chest, her heart felt like it was gathering ice. Feeling numb, she stood and walked away without a backward glance.

As was their tradition for every one of their birthdays, Natasha's friends had made reservations at her favorite restaurant. Natasha didn't want to be there, really, but she knew her friends would worry if she didn't show.

So, she started a bill on drinks and appetizers, and settled in, waiting for her friends to arrive.

It didn't surprise Natasha to see both her friends walk in within seconds of each other.

"Happy B-day," Rusty said, plunking her humongous purse on the seat next to her. "I tried calling you at work but was told you were out for the day. What gives, birthday girl?"

"Hey." Vanessa slid into the booth next to her. "I see the birthday party got started without me."

"No worries. You'll catch up," Natasha said, already feeling the two drinks she'd had.

"So, what did the birthday girl do this year to celebrate this momentous occasion?" Vanessa asked.

Natasha raised her martini glass to toast herself. "I put in my notice at Madison and Madison. I quit."

Rusty's jaw hung open. "No shit?"

"Serious?" Vanessa said at the same time.

"Dead serious."

Vanessa flagged a waiter. "I'll have whatever she's having."

"And I'll take another one, please," Natasha said.

"And I'll take a lemonade," Rusty added.

When he left, Rusty turned toward her. "What brought this on?"

Natasha stirred the olive in her drink, ignoring the well of emotion in her throat. "It's time I did this."

Her friends shared concerned glances.

"But what got you fired up enough to quit?" Vanessa asked.

Natasha ran her fingers over the stem of the glass. "I'm just tired of it, you know? Tired of working so hard at something I really don't want to be. Tired of following what other people expect me to be." She shrugged, then twirled the stem of the glass. "Tired of trying to make my mom proud, which is, by the way, an impossibility."

"I knew it had something to do with her," Vanessa mumbled.

The waiter breezed to their table, served the drinks, and breezed away.

"She only helped bring on the epiphany, you know?" Natasha explained.

"What epiphany?" Vanessa asked.

"That I don't take many risks. It's been easy to let people take control of my life. I was working for my parents, so it's not like they were ever going to fire me. I even let my mom pick out my now-ex-boyfriend. This is it. I need to cut loose."

"Yup, cut loose," Rusty said, sharing another worried glance with Vanessa.

Inexplicably, Natasha felt tears fill her eyes, threatening to spill. Too many drinks and not enough appetizers, she lectured herself. She swallowed past the choke in her throat. "You know, my parents are just looking out for the business. Mom can't help it. Hell, they built it from scratch all those years ago, so I can understand her being protective of it and all. Maybe that's what I need to do now—start something for myself. Something all mine."

"We've got your back, girl," Rusty said with a loyal vengeance that warmed Natasha's heart.

"You bet," Vanessa agreed, clicking her drink to her friends'.

"And if worse comes to worst, I can always use an extra mechanic at the shop," Rusty teased.

"Ditto for the flower shop," Vanessa offered.

The thought echoed in her head long after her friends had left. She felt a little tipsy and had a sudden pressing need to see Logan one last time, to let him know where things stood between them.

If she wrapped it all up with him tonight, she could start tomorrow fresh and new, without ties to him or the law firm.

No point being a coward about it.

Logan was sitting at his desk when the buzzer by his phone alerted him to unusual activity at the front door. Knowing that Ivan wouldn't bother him unless it was important, Logan switched on the main entry camera, expecting to see cops on the premises, a fight about to take place, or some sort of practical joke.

Instead, barely hidden by Ivan's broad shoulders was the unexpected image of Natasha.

Logan clicked the audio feed.

". . . tattoo looks familiar," she said, staring at the identical eagle tattoo Logan's friend had on his shoulder where the muscle shirt didn't hide it.

"Really?" Ivan the Subtle, Logan thought, as he watched Ivan lean forward, probably sniffing her breath for alcohol.

"I'm probably mistaken," she said, smiling disingenuously, but Logan noticed her words were slurring a bit.

"Mind if I get your car keys?" With a burst from a flash, Ivan was already taking her picture for the key tag before she could respond. "We'll set you up with a taxi."

She clutched her purse. "No, thanks. I came in a taxi. Look, I'll only take a minute of Mr. Taylor's time."

"I'm not sure if he's in."

Logan hurriedly pressed the button to let Ivan know he was available.

"But you may be in luck." Ivan nodded to the other bouncer and gestured to Natasha. "This way, please."

Logan switched off the monitor, glanced at the semi-messy room, then hurriedly cleared away all the gnawed-off swizzle sticks that littered his desk and straightened the clutter of paper into a manageable stack.

By the time the polite knock sounded on his door, he was ready. Looking like a muscled butler, Ivan led Natasha into the room, gave a half bow at the door, and left, closing the door behind him.

The big, burly Russian-boxer-look-alike had tried to finagle the keys from Natasha again. Okay, she was tipsy. She got that. But she wasn't planning on driving anywhere. Sheesh!

"Mr. Taylor," she said, still clutching her purse.

"Tasha," he said in greeting. "Benita Madison called."

"Oh?"

"Told me you'd quit."

"She did?"

"Claims she had nothing to do with it."

The low-level headache pulsed harder at the back of Natasha's head. "I did quit."

"Hmm."

What the hell did that mean? "Yes, well, don't worry, the brilliant legal counsel at Madison and Madison is still available to represent your business, should you need it."

He indicated she should sit, and he parked his butt on the corner of the desk. "Why did you quit?"

She shrugged. "I had an epiphany, and realized I'm not cut out for law."

He paused, then walked back to his chair behind the desk and tipped it backward, looking utterly relaxed and lazy. "Your mother is concerned. She didn't let on, but my guess is that she's taking it hard."

Natasha braced against the ache his words brought. "Trust me, they'll do just fine."

"I meant as your mother, not your boss."

Natasha shrugged. "I don't want to talk about it anymore."

"And yet, here you are," he pointed out.

Telling him that she'd quit had seemed so important an hour ago, and now it seemed trivial, something she could've handled with a phone call. "I wanted to let you know, face to face, that you don't have to worry about Madison and Madison."

He didn't say anything, but he frowned slightly, his gaze settling on her lips.

"Well, this has been fun," she said, popping out of her chair. "I'm sure I can find my way out."

But by the time she reached for the doorknob, he was there. He stood close enough for his myriad of scents to engulf her. Glancing down to avoid looking at him, she spotted the small garbage bin by the desk, the dozen or so swizzle sticks at the bottom like emaciated red licorice.

"You should not have kissed me," she blurted.

He exhaled, paused. "It's a good thing we were stopped."

"Yes." She turned the knob, but the flat of his hand held the door closed.

"Want to know why?" he asked.

"No."

She could almost hear his heart beating. "Because I would've taken you right there, swear to God."

Don't say that. No . . . She shook her head. "Fantasy's over. You don't have to do this anymore."

"Maybe it's time to add a taste of reality."

"There is no room for fantasies in reality."

"Wanna bet?" He kissed her, the unexpectedness of it reigniting the smoldering desire that seemed to hover just under the surface. The moment melded so perfectly with the one where she'd had the mangled cigarette in her hand that it seemed no interruption had occurred. His mouth drank, gobbled, and fogged up her mind.

Daring to steal a few more seconds, she got weak-kneed, clutching him for more, surrendering so quickly it cut through all her well-planned defenses.

"No fair," she managed, when they surfaced for air. She tried to brush the feel of the kiss away with one hand while holding him at bay with the other.

She stepped away from him, needing more distance to think. "I never wanted anything remotely complicated. The mystery of being strangers is gone. The Orchid Soul thing is riddled with bugs. And this," she pointed to herself and him, "relationship or whatever it is, doesn't feel simple."

He touched her cheek. "What's so complicated? As far as I can see, it's all simple. Even the white lie I told was simple. The only one making things difficult is you."

"No." She shook her head, emotion thawing out like a frozen bubble inside her. "It may be simple for you, but *not* for me. I quit my job today—a family job, no less. My parents have probably lost respect for me, when all I wanted was to have a secret sex life that no one would know about. Why? Because I wanted to be happy. To see if I really could step out of my comfort zone, find another kind of woman inside me—you know, discover my kinky side. And now . . ." Damn, she sure as hell *was* drunk, babbling on this way. "Fuck it."

She sighed, and he cupped her face as if he intended to kiss her again, but then he changed his mind. Instead, he reached for her purse and had an arm around her before she could protest.

"Come on, Tasha. I'm taking you home."

Shrugging her shoulders didn't work. The feel and scent of him felt too goddamned comforting and safe. As always, being next to him unlocked that deviant part of her that wanted to just grope him just to get her kicks. The other part of her was much more sober. "No, I'll take a cab."

"Why waste your money?"

"Logan—"

"You should call me Mr. Taylor." He gave her another long, hungry look. "I'm not sure I can handle you calling me Logan

right now, because in your condition, I have no business thinking what I'm thinking."

Natasha blew at her bangs. "I don't need you to take care of
me. I can take care of myself."

His voice was a bit gruff as he replied. "Sure, let's stick with
that. You came all the way over here to tell me what's on your
mind. The least I can do is to drive you home."

In the end, he got her to take a few sips of coffee that did
nothing to counteract the alcohol in her bloodstream but left
her tired and melancholy. She gave Logan her address, then
reluctantly got into his sleek convertible hot rod, a vintage she
didn't recognize.

As they left, the bouncer with the similar tattoo raised a
questioning eyebrow at Logan but did little more than wave.

Logan's hot rod was a beast, deep-throated, with wide tires
and geared to whip through curves like a roller coaster. Natasha
felt the night whiz by her, the wind teasing her hair to the point
of rebellion. Neon signs, stop lights, and headlights smeared
their colors, painting everything like a surreal dream.

"Turn left there," she directed him. "Then a right at the
stop sign."

The closer she got to her house, the more sober she felt. If
she asked him in, would he think it was the alcohol talking? Was
it wrong to want to spend the night together, just one last time?

Much too soon, he parked in her driveway. Nosy Mrs. Morris across the street still had her living room light on, the careful shift of her curtains giving her away.

He killed the engine, but neither of them moved to open
the doors.

"Come inside," she found herself saying.

He sighed, looked off across the street to Mrs. Morris's, then back. "What happened to keeping things simple? You're sending mixed messages, Tasha."

Hell, he was right. She ran her hands over her frazzled hair. "Sorry. I guess I'm just not thinking straight."

And still neither of them moved for a moment. Then he pressed a button, and the convertible rooftop began to rise, locking into place.

"Okay." He looked at her.

"Okay?" Just like that?

"Yup." He waited, the final decision clearly left up to her.

There was relief in not having to defend her waffling or even to rationalize that she was once again stepping in the wrong direction. "All right, then. Come on in."

She stepped out of the car, closed the door, and unzipped her purse to search for the key to her front door.

Logan followed Natasha into her home, his hands sliding into his front pockets once they were inside.

Nothing was messy or out of place. In fact, the place look like it existed in a dust-free bubble. The white and black décor was a bit unnerving though. Where was the burst of colors he had been expecting?

She kicked off her shoes, setting them by the front door, then placed her hefty purse on the foyer table. Her aim was slightly off and the purse tipped, falling to the ground and spilling its contents.

"Shit." She scrambled after the items, and as he reached down to help, he spotted the recorder he'd given her of the stairwell sex. A bottle of headache pills rolled against it, and not far from that was a jewelry box whose label he easily recognized. Falling from the box was a string of white pearls that he bet cost a mint.

Nail polish, lipstick, a wallet, and a compact were quickly scooped up and tucked back into the purse.

"You keep the sex recording in your purse?"

She reached for the medicine and avoided his gaze. "I never got around to putting it away."

Sweet lie. "What about this?" He held up the jewelry box. "It's no trinket."

"Birthday gift," she mumbled, snatching it from him and setting it on the table.

"Aha. Well, happy birthday."

She frowned and kept gathering her things again. "Those two words don't belong together. Besides, my mother gave me that a few days ago anyway."

"You've been carrying this in your purse for days? It looks like something you oughta get insured."

She huffed and tossed at least three packages of gum into her purse. "Shackles."

He frowned, getting confused. "The gum or the—"

"The necklace," she said between her gritting teeth. "It's my mother's idea of a gift, but really, they're just shackles. It's meant to remind me that she has money, and that money buys things,-affords luxuries. So, every birthday, I get reminders. And I wear them to work, to dinner, and to every event they host, just to let them know I haven't forgotten, and—God, I cannot shut up!"

She closed her eyes briefly, then sighed. "Forget it. I'm . . . working out a few issues. Pretend I didn't say any of that."

Like that would happen.

When she finished picking up the remaining items, she zipped the purse and placed it squarely on the table next to the jewelry box.

He tried to keep his mouth shut, knowing she'd read too much into it, but he asked anyway. "Want to talk about it?"

"No."

She looked annoyed and frustrated, and he wondered if she was about to kick him out.

"Mind if I take a quick shower?" she asked, already heading off to where he assumed was a bathroom. "Help yourself to whatever's in the fridge or the cupboards or whatever."

Escaping, he realized.

Hell, he'd pushed a button she didn't want pushed, but frankly, whatever issues she had with her mother were also affecting them.

Left on his own, he shrugged off his jacket, made two cups of peppermint tea he found in her pantry, turned on her nearby stereo system, then sat back and savored one while he waited for her return, but as he did so, he found himself glancing at her purse.

Why would she carry around a gift that drove her crazy? What did it mean that she also carried around their audio sex tape? Giving in to temptation, he retrieved the jewelry box sitting next to the purse, taking out the gleaming string of white pearls.

I just want to be happy. Her words haunted him, stirred something in him. Inexplicably, he wanted to fix whatever it was that made her lonely, that made her carry around a fortune in pearls as if they were worth more than her happiness. And what did that say about their flesh-for-fantasy recordings?

I just want to be happy. He could make her happy, couldn't he? Just a little?

"Snooping, are we?" Somehow, he'd failed to notice that she was standing by the door, her black silk robe draping over her curves like water, disapproval and wariness emanating from her like a force. She stood with such stillness, almost fragility, that time seemed to stop.

He held the pearls in the palm of his hand. "Just taking a closer look."

She crossed her arms.

He set the pearls down on the couch. Ah, so he'd crossed her line again. Maybe it was time he pulled her over to his side, just for a bit. "Come here."

"Why?"

"Just come here."

When she stood close enough, he put his hands at her waistline. "When I was a kid, we couldn't afford much. It seemed like all the other families had the video games and such, but not us. Ivan's mom would get tired of us complaining, so she'd tell us to go in the backyard and spin."

"Spin?"

The memory tugged a grin from him. "That's right. We'd spin like fools until we ran into each other and then fall on the ground laughing."

He took a step, tugging her so she followed in a half-spin.

"Logannnn . . ." Natasha stiffened but followed his lead. He ignored her warning tone.

"When was the last time you spun around?" He turned again, but with her in his arms, it was almost like dancing.

"Oh, no. Stop. Logan? I'm not going to spiiiin!" Laughter

escaped her as he spun her again, her feet not even touching the ground.

"You're not?" He spun her faster, delighted to hear her giggle. "But, my robe!"

"Never mind your robe."

He spun her some more, hearing her mild complaints and half-giggles, the silky robe slipping and sliding open. "I'm not entirely sober, you know. I could get dizzy and nauseated, and then this could get realllly messy!" But she was grinning widely, lost in the whirlwind. "Logan!"

"Tasha." But he was laughing, too.

She kept her eyes tightly shut, as if worried she'd get dizzier with her eyes open.

"Stop, oh, stop!" But she was holding on tight. "If you keep going, I swear I'm going to throw up."

"Can't have that." He slowed until her feet touched the ground again. "There."

"You. Are. Totally crazy!"

"And you look . . . happy."

She opened her eyes to see his braids still swaying, his wide mischievous smile beaming as the whirlwind came to an end. She probably did look happy, she realized. The childish activity made her feel absurdly giddy all the way to her toes, but it was the attentive look in his eyes that revealed how much he genuinely wanted to see her happy. Her heart fumbled through a few irregular heartbeats at the beautiful, dangerous thought.

"I could've spun myself around," she pointed out.

"Yup. So why don't you?"

"Because I'm an adult."

"What's that got to do with anything?"

She wanted to sink her hands into his hair, to curl into him and be spun around again. Instead, she cleared her throat. "You do see how this would present a problem in public, right?"

"There's no law against it."

"Imagine that . . ."

He lowered his head in degrees, as if expecting her to retaliate, but she didn't. The touch of his lips on hers was slow and sensual, his tongue coaxing her mouth open, kissing her at a slow-burning pace that molded his mouth on hers, his peppermint against her spearmint toothpaste. The tongue-tangling kisses brought back the vortex of sensations all over again, like slow dancers, for what felt like an eternity.

Before she knew it, he'd settled down on the couch and put her on his lap, his hands shifting over the silky robe, rubbing gently against her skin.

Between her thighs, she could feel his erection taking shape as she ate his mouth up like luscious, melting ice cream. She explored at her own pace, waiting to become completely breathless before testing the length of his neck and the bristly burr of his jaw, before again savoring his mouth.

She was so caught up in the slow seduction that it took her a moment to realize he'd pushed her hands behind her back— not to take the robe off but to wrap the string of pearls like handcuffs around her wrists.

Like shackles.

"God, Logan, don't."

"Shh," he admonished. "Careful. These are heirloom pearls. Would it be the end of the world if the necklace broke?"

"Yes!"

"Then don't break it." He kissed her before she could protest again. But with her first breath, she was already saying his name.

"Shh. Trust me, Tasha."

His wide hands moved up her thighs, dragging silk, scattering her apprehension as his lips found her left breast, nipping the softness of her skin before taking it into the warmth of his mouth.

His hands settled on her hips, pulling her toward him. She stiffened, belatedly hearing the grit and strain of pearls rubbing together. She tried to recover, to work up some sort of anger, but his eyes held her, defeating the battle before it began.

"Careful," he whispered, continuing to suck and tease her breast.

As he moved to the other breast, his hand shifted in the silk of her robe again, moving down to where the robe pooled in her lap. He had her nipple tenuously between his teeth when his hand shifted over the silk and rubbed lazily against her clit, grazing over her wet pussy.

Pearls creaked.

She cussed under her breath.

He winked and moved his hand again, knuckles over silk, rolling over her clit like soft licks.

"Logan . . ." She wiggled a bit on his lap, anticipating his hardness, remembering the familiar thick length of him and restless to have him slide into her again and again. . . .

But he took his time, the slow-paced rhythm of strokes making the material slick and slippery, building up a quiver deep inside her vagina that had her dancing against the rub with a hunger that turned her voice into moans. "Logan . . . fuck . . ."

His kiss was just a bit harder, almost punishing, and his knuckled caresses became fisted curls against her mons that had her panting shamelessly. Abruptly the move changed to long fingers that tugged, stroked, and rubbed the wet silk over the folds of her sex, without penetrating.

"Logan, please, please . . . Oh, God . . ."

With every spike and strain, the pearls pushed tightly against her wrists, creaking.

"I need you inside me," she whispered. "Please."

"Yes." *Anything you want.*

His hands abandoned her for his zipper, whipping out a condom from his back pocket, putting it on, then readjusting her on his lap.

His hands clamped down on her hips, guiding her over his erection and lowering her, pushing his cock into her hot, wet sex until she was gripping him with her tight muscles.

They both groaned in pleasure and took a moment to savor the start. Each stroke over her clit had her tensing around his cock, each roll of his hips was matched by hers as she bounced on his lap.

"Tasha." Sweet God, he was so close. Their mouths devoured each other, demanding more. He rolled his thumb over the wet satin covering her clit just as he sucked her neck at the tender spot that always gave her shivers.

That was all it took for her to fall apart.

Her raw cry mingled with the sound of a snap, followed by a burst of bouncing pearls scattering and falling all over her wooden floor.

Blindly, she clung and rode him, her thighs gripping him, milking him, feeding the riptide release that almost brought tears to her eyes.

He also moved within her, thrusting into her over and over, his ejaculation mirrored in the tightening of his fingers, in his harsh, hard grunt and abrupt gush of breath.

"Tasha—"

She clenched her fingers into his hair, hiding her face next to his neck, his pulse thundering against her ear. The silk robe was half parted, and in places their skin touched. In others, her perspiration made the robe clingy.

Seconds drifted by, slow as molasses.

His hands moved under her robe, roaming over her back. "Happy birthday."

Her sigh came from deep in her soul, as if she'd stripped something away, and yet . . . "I broke the necklace."

His lips brushed over her temple, his eyes making fleeting contact with hers. "I should say I'm sorry, but I'm not. I promise I'll get the necklace fixed."

"No, that's okay." She hadn't expected to feel so relieved. So incredibly free. She'd never be able to think of pearls in the same way again.

"Are you okay?" he asked.

"Never better."

Still on his lap, she shifted just enough to tug gently at his sparse chest hair. Goddammit, he'd known what he was doing, she realized. Part of her was clamoring to thank him for it.

"You missed your calling, Logan Taylor. You should've been a psychologist," she mumbled.

He made an innocuous rumbling sound that vibrated in his chest and into her ear. "Not sure what you mean."

She peered up at him, catching the telltale look that passed over his face. "Yes, you do."

He shrugged, waited a few seconds. "Most days, the only difference between a bartender and a psychologist is the hourly pay."

"Never thought of it that way."

"Want to grab another necklace?" he asked with a cheeky grin.

"Once was more than enough."

She sat up, ran her hands over his shoulders. He'd taken a risk, not knowing if it would backfire on him. Not for his sake, but for hers. It was unexpectedly heartwarming.

"Remind me to hurt you later," she teased.

A slow, fearless grin formed. "I have such a bad memory, but, okay. I'll try."

Natasha had no idea a person could be so creative with a single pearl. Of course, when it came to creativity and sex, Logan trumped any past lover.

He had chased a fat pearl around her clit like a billiard ball routing to a hidden corner pocket. As if that wasn't enough, he licked it up and down her sensitive labia with his tongue, playing the slippery bead in and out of her pussy until she was gripping the bedsheets in her hands and damn near howling for mercy.

How he didn't accidentally swallow the gem, she didn't know.

His tongue, teeth, and mouth took her to the edge, the click of the pearl against his teeth burning into her memory, the hum of his lips against her becoming almost as devastating as the velvety stroke of his tongue when he lapped her up.

And even after she came, shamelessly holding his face to her shuddering pussy, she couldn't deny him when he spoke in her ear. "I need you."

"Have me," she replied.

The length of his cock slid into her wetness even though she was too limp to move. His rigid, deep thrusts renewed ripples of pleasure in her aftermath, and she arched and wrapped her legs around him until he too found his orgasm.

Nine ❦

Logan felt like he was on vacation.

Wearing only his jeans, he whipped up eggs for breakfast. Earlier, he'd gathered all the pearls and placed them in a bowl by Natasha's purse. He tried to ignore them, but no matter how he turned, he could see their reflection caught in the stainless steel toaster, reminding him of the night's events.

He hadn't planned on spending the entire night, but here he was.

Things were getting pretty personal, and truth be told, he couldn't stop dreaming up ways to make her happy. He wanted to see her smile and laugh, and damned if he wasn't feeling just a touch obsessive about it.

Logan had just finished pouring the coffee in the mugs when Natasha shuffled into the kitchen, wearing only his shirt and looking like a ruffled sex kitten.

"Morning," she said, peering at him through bleary eyes.

"Or brunch time," he corrected, pushing a mug of coffee across the kitchen counter to her. "Omelette okay?"

"God, yes. I thought I was dreaming it. It smells amazing." She took a dainty sip of the steaming coffee, pausing to relish it.

With a smile, she scooted onto the counter stool, forked a hefty slice of the omelette into her mouth, then gobbled it with a greediness that made him glad he'd stayed. Logan leaned forward against the counter from her, satisfied to eat in silence and just watch her. The lack of conversation should've felt awkward, but it didn't.

"So," she said, after the last of the egg was gone, "How come you and the bouncer have the same tattoo?"

The unexpected question caught him off guard. The fact that it was personal was an even bigger surprise.

"He's my brother."

She frowned. "Brother?"

He rubbed his bristly jaw, wondering how much personal info to reveal. "We don't share the same DNA, but we're blood brothers. His parents raised me when I was a teen, and we've been a family ever since. He's Ivan."

Her eyes grew more alert. "So you went out and got the same tattoo?"

"Yup."

"Why?"

He paused, not sure what to make of her pursuing the personal conversation. "Pops got it first, so we figured we would too."

"It's interesting that you have the two flags. I take it your brother is Russian?"

Logan gulped more coffee. "Ivan's Russian. He became a citizen a while back."

"Ah."

They sipped the coffee, and he realized she wasn't going to discuss their night together.

"If you wait just a bit, I can give you your shirt back," she said.

He walked around, then reached for her, letting his hands roam under the hem, over the softness of her skin, mildly surprised to find she'd put on some underwear. He brushed his lips over hers, their coffee breaths mingling.

"No, keep it." His hands roamed, her nipples were firm and hard against his palms. "Your robe is out of commission anyway."

She leaned up and kissed him, their mouths tangling for a long moment.

From outside, the sound of a car pulling up to her driveway caught his attention. "I think you've got company."

Natasha reluctantly moved away from him to peer out the kitchen window. Her emphatic, "Crap," confirmed his suspicion.

As luck would have it, Benita Madison had decided to pay her daughter a visit.

Natasha turned and started toward her room to grab her robe, then remembered it was too soiled from the night's sex play. Frantically, she looked around the room, remembering the disarray of the night before and scanning quickly to make sure none of the pearls were around.

Beside her, Logan stood as still as an oak tree, and she suddenly remembered that his car was still parked outside, a fact that her mother was not going to miss.

The knock came sooner than she'd expected. As if jolted by lightning, Natasha ran into her bedroom, threw on a pair of jeans, and struggled with a bra until she realized it was twisted and knotted. In her haste to straighten it, her thumb ripped through the lace cup, and in frustration, she flung it down. Okay, so she'd be braless. Not a *really* big deal.

"Shit, shit, shit!" she grumbled as she hurried back into the living room, finding Logan leaning against the counter in the same spot, sipping his coffee as if disaster wasn't about to strike.

And why not look calm? What point was there in outrunning the storm?

He even had the nerve to wink at her when she finally headed for the front door.

"Good morning, Mother," she greeted, not opening the door the whole way or inviting her in.

Her mother lowered her dark sunglasses, her frown putting a strain in what was usually a smooth, youthful appearance. "Try afternoon, dear. Mind if I come in?"

"Actually—"

Benita simply barged in. As the door swung wider, a marblelike sound caught their attention, and they both looked down to see a pearl rolling across the wooden floor, stopping just a few feet away from where Logan was relaxing against the kitchen counter, sipping his blessed coffee.

"Good afternoon," he greeted in mock cheerfulness.

Benita absorbed it all—zeroing in on Natasha's lack of a

bra, Logan's near nakedness, the cozy little morning-after ambience. Her brow furrowed further when she spotted the bowl
of loose pearls on the foyer table.

An odd mixture of hurt and dejection crossed Benita's face,
surprising Natasha, only to be replaced by a blast of animosity.
The clipped, "Good afternoon, Mr. Taylor," sounded a lot like
"Burn in hell, you son-of-a-bitch."

Logan looked as at ease in his lack of clothing as he would've
in a tuxedo. The look in her mother's eyes had Natasha standing between them.

"You should've called," she said to her mother, hoping to
soften the reproach with a stiff smile.

"I did call. Your father called as well. Twice. But perhaps
you were too busy entertaining to pick up."

Oh, double crap!

"I was." She could feel her cheeks flushing, but she forged
on. "Busy, that is." She glanced at Logan for help, but he only
winked back.

"Coffee?" he asked Benita.

Her mother's eyes were almost lethal. "No, thank you. I
thought we had an agreement, Mr. Taylor?"

"No, *you* thought we had an agreement."

Natasha gripped her mug tighter. "What's going on?"

Her mother ignored her. "Under these circumstances, I
must inform you that Madison and Madison will no longer be
representing you or your businesses."

Natasha almost dropped her coffee. "You cannot be serious."

But Logan was already agreeing. "Understood."

"Well, *I* don't understand!" Natasha said, glancing from one to the other. "I'm no longer working for you, Mom, so how does my association with him affect your ability to represent him?"

Benita's focus turned to Natasha. "I'm having trouble understanding why you've made the decisions you have been making." Her eyes narrowed. "Quitting your job. Then *cavorting* in alleyways like some—"

"Enough!" Natasha's tone hit with the force of a shotgun, making the following silence almost deafening. She couldn't tell who was more surprised. Herself or her mother.

"Mom, I think you should leave."

Benita's eyebrows shot up, and for a few seconds they squared off. "Yes, I believe I will."

Reshouldering her purse, Benita turned her eyes to the bowl of pearls. "If you didn't like the birthday present, all you had to do was say so."

Shiiit!

Without a backward glance, Benita turned and left, not bothering to close the door when she made her exit. A rush of pettiness had Natasha slamming it shut.

She took a deep breath, finding Logan still sipping his coffee, his face unreadable.

Natasha brushed hair from her face. "I'm sorry."

He seemed to consult with the steam in his coffee before speaking. "I can see where she's coming from. She's your mom, and she's concerned about you. Here you are, behaving scandalously, cavorting with—"

"Stop with that word. I don't cavort."

"We cavorted plenty last night."

She crossed her arms, trying to hide her breasts as she puffed in a breath of denial. "Whose side are you on, Logan?"

"Yours, of course." Natasha didn't know what to make of the glint of humor sneaking back in his eyes.

"You don't seem overly upset that you were just dropped by Madison and Madison," she noted.

"I don't like ultimatums. Even from the best."

"So, what did she say? Stop dating my daughter or else?"

Logan set his empty mug down. "Not in those words exactly, but close enough."

Natasha sighed, the bowl of pearls catching her attention for a moment. "I usually lead a very simple, organized life. I don't understand why my mother is behaving this way. Orchid Soul was just for fun. I didn't expect it to affect your business life."

"No worries." He absently tugged his ear. "You know, I hardly ever get what I want in life without things getting messy somehow, so I'm used to it. But maybe you're not. . . . Maybe this is about as messy as you want to get. And if so, I understand."

Could he truly just walk away from it? "Is that how you feel? You want to walk away from this?"

"No." He ran a hand over his naked chest, mumbling, "Look, I don't want to stand between you and your parents. I'm trying to be—what's the word?—noble?"

He looked so uncomfortable about what he said regarding family that she knew he was serious.

She crossed her arms, instinctively protecting a fragile, naked hope that quivered in her chest.

"I shouldn't have to pick between you or them," she stated.

"Then don't." Their gazes locked, his prying eyes probably finding answers she didn't want to give.

"Okay." Maybe he had a point.

Seven hard, thundering heartbeats later, he nodded. "I have to get back to work."

When he went in search of his jacket, her eyes drifted to the single pearl gleaming on the floor. She picked it up and placed it in the bowl with the others.

She stood with her hands cupping the bowl as he walked behind her. There was a slight pause in his stride, then his hand barely brushed her hip, as if he meant to turn her around. She looked over her shoulder at him.

If he'd meant to say anything, he must've changed his mind. Instead, he dropped a brief kiss on her cheek, and by the time she opened her eyes, he was gone.

It wasn't until his car was purring down the street that she realized she was still wearing his T-shirt.

Ten ✿

Natasha changed into tank top and shorts, doubled up on some gum, and for the next few hours went a little overboard on the cleaning spree.

She cornered every dust bunny, polished every wooden, glass, porcelain, steel, and tile surface of her home until it gleamed, then went extra ballistic scrubbing, mopping and vacuuming until she'd worked up a hard, shirt-clinging sweat and the house was as spotless as it had ever been.

At one point, she found herself in her closet, suddenly deciding that she really didn't need half her clothes. The old, stodgy business suits were out. So were the comfy old jogging suits and worn-out yoga pants. And, hell, there were clothes that were ten years old that she was just not going to wear anymore. Caught in the frenzy, she tossed out any pair of shoes that pinched her toes after three hours. Then she raided her makeup drawer and practically emptied it. Out, all of it!

Today, she was turning over a new leaf.

By the time she turned away from the closet, there was a small mountain of clothes and shoes in the middle of her bedroom floor. And it felt *good*.

She packed whatever was decent enough to donate to the local thrift store and trashed the items that deserved to be tossed.

Feeling a bit more focused and revived, she went into the kitchen and poured a tall glass of iced tea, then downed it, looking around with pride, noticing for the first time that the duo-tones of black and white lacked the vibrancy she suddenly craved. That would change soon.

Time to make a fresh, new start. One thing at a time.

After putting the empty glass in the sink, her eyes landed on her desk nook where her laptop rested. What was she going to do about Logan? Or her parents?

He had begun as a secret project, a sexy risk. But it had turned into more, at least for her.

And, true, his biggest appeal initially was his damned sexiness. But he'd gone noble, and that, in its own way, was even more sexy.

There was a part of her that wanted to know more about his brother and the surrogate Russian family. She wanted to know more about him as a man. She wanted to understand the man behind the façade he displayed so well. The man who knotted pearls around her wrists and spun her around in circles, unraveled emotions she could hardly put into words.

No, she wasn't going to give him up. Not yet. If he was

trouble and things got messy, so be it. He wasn't the reason for the problems between her and her mother. Truth be told, he was the final straw in a long list of things.

She had to find a way to tell her parents that.

Having showered and toweled off, she dressed and headed for the answering machine, listening first to her mother's oddly cautious and abrupt message, followed by the more patient request from her father for her to call him.

She dialed her father first. He picked up on the first ring.

"Hi, sweetheart." Even as he greeted her, she could hear his second line start ringing in the background. "You had us worried last night, Natasha. What's this I hear about you quitting?"

She momentarily closed her eyes. "Dad, I have to do this. I think it's time for something new."

"Something new." He spoke in a calm voice, like a scientist puzzling over a chemical solution. "How much of this decision is based on Mr. Logan Taylor?"

She leaned against the wall. If there was anyone she dreading discussing her sex life with . . . "I don't know what to tell you, Dad, except that Mr. Taylor isn't the driving reason behind my decision. I thought I could do it, you know? I thought that if I tried enough, I'd be a great attorney like you and Mom, but I don't have it in me."

He paused. "You don't have the passion for it," he said, his tone resigned.

"I can honestly say that I gave it my best shot, Dad."

He paused. "I've guess I've kinda known for some time. Believe it or not, your mom and I both want what's best for you. If it's not here, then," he exhaled, "go out and find it. You have my blessing."

A weight seemed to lift from her chest.

"But baby girl, about Mr. Taylor, I hope you'll be careful."

She rolled her eyes. "Dad, I know what I'm doing."

He sighed, the sound of it backed by the insistent ringing of his second line. "It seems like just yesterday that you had pigtails and you were busy terrorizing my office. And yes, I know you are an adult now, one who—well, you know—has relations and all that."

"Relations?" She chuckled, but he was already rushing the words together, as if he could hardly speak them.

"This is not the easiest conversation in the world for me, but I'm trying to keep an open mind."

She bit her lip. "Okay, Dad."

"All right then." She could suddenly envision him doing his persuasive hand gesture that indicated he was back on track. "Look, I know Eugene hurt you. You deserve someone better this time around—someone who will respect you, take care of you, stand by you."

And make me happy? "I know."

"Okay, enough on that." Again the insistent ringing of his second line pulsed in the background. "About your mother, she, ah, she's going through a hard time. Promise me you'll call and talk to her."

Natasha winced. "I'll call tomorrow."

"Call her today."

She winced. "We'll see."

"Natasha. It's important. It's not about Mr. Taylor. There are things you don't know about. Things she doesn't want me to tell you, so that's all I'll say."

She frowned.

"Just call her. Tomorrow at the latest. And please, be patient. For me?"

Since he rarely asked for a favor, she acquiesced. "Okay, I'll call."

By the time she'd hung up, she was already dreading the call she'd promised to make.

Eleven ❧

It was well past midnight when the knock sounded on Logan's door. He gripped the pen he was using to make notes, trying to do the same with his patience.

"What?" He all but barked it.

Ivan poked his head in, bringing with him the loud punching syncopation of the latest band's mad drummer and the wailing rock guitars half a building away.

Business was damned near to overflowing, which meant Ivan should've had better things to do than to show up with a gift-wrapped box in his hand.

"Shouldn't you be cracking heads or something?" Logan asked.

"Special delivery, boss."

"How many times have I told you not to call me that?"

"What am I supposed to call you? Should I resurrect the

old, beloved nickname, Scooter?" Ivan didn't so much as crack a smile, but his eyes were twinkling.

"You looking to get fired?"

"No, boss—um, sir—um, Scooter."

"Ivan, I swear to God."

"Why so uptight? You either need to seriously get laid or you need to chain-smoke a pack of cigarettes. Both are off limits, huh?"

"That does it. You're fired." The absurdity was that he would never do so. It was practically a joke between them.

"But speaking of smoking packages, guess who made the delivery?"

Logan leaned back in his chair, reluctantly biting down on his frustration. "Looks to me like my nosy-ass brother, who I most certainly would not call a smoking package."

Ivan gave a half chuckle. "*I am* a hot smoking package, but I was referring to your lady friend."

My lady friend. An immature thrill almost had him grinning. "Oh?"

"Look at you." Ivan flashed the first real grin Logan had seen in a while, then ruined the moment by making a pretend whipping sound.

Pussy-whipped? "Pssh! Oh, please. Is that how you talk to your employer? I'm seriously considering docking your pay."

Not worried one bit, Ivan scratched his cheek in amusement, shrugged as if to say, "Whatever," then placed the gift on the desk. "Denial. A river. Egypt."

"Get out."

"I could open it for you," Ivan said, shaking the box as if to determine what was inside it. "Could be she put anthrax in there or something else just as deadly."

"Ivan."

"You pay me to do security. I'm just sayin'."

"Out!"

Ivan grinned. "Aha. Sex toys. I understand. No, no. I won't tell a soul." With a wiggle of his brows, Ivan headed out.

Logan waited only long enough to be sure Ivan wouldn't step back in, then carefully tugged off the bow. Gifts were so rare in his life that he took his time with the wrapping paper, making sure he didn't tear the swirling silver and gold design.

Finally, he lifted the lid on the medium-sized box to reveal half of it crammed with thin, red swizzle sticks. Logan chuckled at the sight, ran his hand over them, then grabbed one and stuck it in his mouth.

He craved her like a long hard pull from a cigarette, wanted to feel her breath hot and urgent against his lips, as sultry as smoke. He wanted her against his tongue, to swirl, to savor like mouth-watering cognac. And the cravings weren't getting weaker.

He could hardly wait to get his hands on her.

The other contents in the box turned out to be a tiny Web camera setup, complete with hookup instructions. In a small sterile sandwich bag, he found the remote control to the Clit Clip. Like the horny dog that it was, his cock started swelling in his pants.

Tucked in the middle was handwritten note that simply stated, "I got your Orchid Soul request. Want to play? Tune in tomorrow night."

Logan vaguely remembered writing a fantasy involving an Internet camera and private access. It had been little more than a customized porn fantasy.

But now that Orchid Soul seemed to magically be back in

working order, Tasha was offering to take him up on it. It felt damned good to know she'd decided to pick him over her parents. Or at least, he hoped so.

He rubbed his face, wondering if the last dregs of coffee in the pot would hold him for another couple of hours.

Eyeing the box again, he couldn't explain why he would've settled for a box of stirring sticks without the Web camera. Whatever Web fantasy he'd had at the time hadn't taken into consideration the intimate all-consuming passion of physically being with her, touching her, feeling her skin against his, hearing her sighs and moans up close and personal.

Hell, going along with the webcam would feel a lot like taking a step backward. Like she was distancing herself from him, maybe more than just physically. Keeping things less personal.

He trailed his fingers over the tips of the stirrers before selecting one. His feelings for her were becoming so damned confusing. This type of fantasy was in every man's wet dream. What the hell was wrong with him?

"I want to eat a whole steaming plate of Pelmeni," Ivan announced.

Logan glanced his brother, wondering what had brought on the new topic. They were headed toward the local clinic in relative silence and, frankly, the subject of food was a bit unexpected.

"Mom call or something?" Since their parents had retired to Florida, the weekly phone call was all it took to stay in touch.

"No. I miss her cooking, though."

"Me, too."

Logan hadn't expected to have a heart-to-heart with Ivan about the rough life in prison, but who knew? The man wasn't getting his privates checked for kicks. In prison, there was undoubtedly a number of ways to develop health issues. They'd gone through some preliminary health tests when Ivan had become a bouncer, and although this was a process he had to go through as his employer, Logan figured it likely had more to do with Ivan's desire to date again.

"You look like you've got stuff on your mind. You okay?" he asked, not glancing at him.

"Fine."

That didn't mean much. When they'd been sixteen, Ivan had skateboarded off a rail the wrong way and broken his arm in two places. His answer had been the same then.

"You can talk to me, you know?" Logan said, keeping his eyes glued to the road. Peripherally, he saw Ivan look at him, then look away. "I got a few tips that would improve your Don Juan lifestyle."

Ivan just grinned and shook his head. "Thanks, but, ah, no thanks. I've got this."

"All right. But you know you can talk to me, right? About anything."

"Yeah, I know. Thanks." A few seconds drifted by before Ivan sighed and sucked at his teeth. "So, you have the Pelmeni recipe?"

Logan smiled, reluctantly allowing him to change the subject. "Shit. You used to drive Mom crazy 'cause you would never follow the recipe."

"Recipes are guidelines. I just need the basics."

"Save yourself a visit from the fire department and order out."

Ivan chuckled. "Keep talking shit."

"You couldn't even make chicken taste like chicken," Logan said with a grin.

"I can out-cook you anytime. Name the time and place and be ready to bring it."

"All I'm bringing is antacids."

"Sheeet. Save them for that damned black liquid at work that you call coffee. And what's with putting salt in your coffee? It's bad enough you put it on all your food, but coffee? Try sugar."

"It enhances the flavor."

"Bullshit. It tastes like piss."

"I wouldn't know."

Ivan winged him on the head, but Logan was pulling into the parking lot of the clinic, and like a dimmed switch, the levity faded and the mood got serious again. Ivan wiped his hands against his thighs in a rare show of nerves.

Logan parked the car and Ivan's hand went to the door handle.

"I'll be back in a few," he said as he got out of the car.

"I'll be right here," Logan promised.

Ivan gave him a tentative smile, then walked into the clinic.

Logan reclined his seat a bit and was watching the sliding doors where Ivan had disappeared when he spotted Benita Madison walking from one of the attached hospital buildings. Her head was down, her shoulders hunched, and she was wiping tears from her face with a tissue.

He sat up, his hand drifting to open the door before he caught himself.

Had she been looking up, he knew she would've seen him. As it was, she hurried by, oblivious to everything but her need to get to her car, which wasn't far from his. Once there, she rested her head on the steering wheel for a good two minutes before backing out and driving off.

Oh, great. He glanced at the rearview mirror. Was he supposed to tell Tasha what he'd seen, or did she know?

He peered at the building he'd seen Benita come out of.

Was it his place to bring it up to Natasha? And if so, when? During foreplay, or afterward? he mocked himself. Hell, they were barely getting to be friends.

Twelve ✣

It was Orchid Soul night again.

Natasha glanced at the time again, then looked around the bedroom. Ten minutes left. She'd set up the camera on a cheap tripod she'd bought that morning and followed every painstaking instruction to make sure that the online feed would go only to Logan's computer.

The little touches she'd put around her bedroom for ambience seemed more gaudy than classy. There were three lace fans she'd found on sale and placed on her dresser, not to mention a number of bright silk shawls that she'd draped against her headboard and various other places.

Her black Chinese plush chair would serve as her "Do Me seat," she decided. There were enough lamps angled toward the chair to give her a tan by the end of the session.

For the occasion, she wore a lacy red and black lingerie

top, and an eye patch of a thong that was becoming overly ambitious—as Vanessa had once said, "'twas moving on up."

Five minutes. Her heart pounded with a mixture of dread, excitement, and nervousness. Never in a million years would she have thought she'd be putting on an online porn show!

She tapped her pencil on the notepad then marked things off her final checklist.

One bottled water. Check. When she got nervous, she got thirsty. Ergo the water. Not that she'd guzzle it with him watching, but it was nice to know it was going to be nearby.

Peach-scented lubricant. Check. It had been the only scented lubricant at the drugstore. And since it was the fifth drugstore she'd visited for the same reason, she'd bought it.

Towels. Check. There was no reason for them, other than simple cleanliness. It just seemed like another appropriate thing to have handy. Oh, maybe she'd splash herself with some bottled water for erotic effect. Or not.

Twisting her lips in thought, she put a question mark next to the checkmark.

Music. Check. She'd bought the best of Barry White. If it wasn't the soundtrack to all online porn, it should've been, hands down. Well, there was that stairwell recording . . . No, no! Barry would do.

Lipstick. Check. She might as well cross it off, but having an extra item on the list seemed to substantiate it.

Two minutes.

She put the notepad away and settled into the chair to wait, quickly making sure her phone was still on. It reminded her that her mother had yet to reply to her voice mail message. Heck, she'd deal with that later.

But now what? What was Logan going to be like? Would he ask her to pose? To do a cyber lap dance? To masturbate upon his instruction?

Would he assume she'd add toys to the list? After all, she *had* given him back the remote control to the Clit Clip. Everything was in place and ready to go.

But it didn't feel right. Not entirely. She didn't want him to be across town watching her. She wanted him there, with her, where she could touch him and seduce him in person.

As her mental counter wound down to five, four, and three, she impulsively reached over and disconnected her computer from the Internet.

Feeling giddy and incredibly juvenile, she waited a minute more, then almost jumped out of her skin when the phone rang.

She answered at mid-ring. "Hello?"

"This thing's not working," Logan spoke, without introduction. "I'm putting in the IP numbers you gave me and I'm getting a connection error."

That's because I've sabotaged it! She rolled her eyes and bit her lip before asking, "What do you mean? Did you recheck your cables?"

"Yes, everything is on."

"And you're sure you're connected to the Internet?"

"It's the first thing I checked. Want to check my IP address?"

"Sure, read the numbers off."

He did. She pretended to be stumped. For the next five minutes, they tried several other things, but still the error persisted.

"Well, that's bizarre. I don't know what to say," she finally mumbled.

She could hear him scratching his jaw. "Well, hell. Do you have a plan B?"

Natasha looked around at all her prep work. Plan B? "Nope. No contingency plan."

The pause began to get lengthy.

"Technology sucks. Why don't I just come over and you can pretend I'm halfway around the world instead of across from you?"

Perfect! She nervously nibbled her lip, wondering if she was really fooling him. "Are you sure? I mean, I hate to inconvenience you, but, um, if you're up for it—"

His chuckle said it all. "See you in twenty minutes." Then he hung up.

She sprang into action, moving the lamps back to their original spots and removing some of the bright shawls from the furniture.

When the phone rang again, she hurried to pick it up, wondering what last-minute request he was going to have for her.

"Hello?"

It took Natasha a moment to identify the voice on the phone as her mother's. "Hi."

"I was just returning your call. . . . Is now a bad time?"

Terrible! "No, no. It's fine."

"I was wondering if you were available for dinner tonight. I think there are a few things I'd like to discuss with you."

"Mom—"

"I'll be sure to keep it brief."

"I kinda had plans—"

"Please."

The last word had Natasha taking a deep breath and sitting down on her bed. "Okay. When and where?"

Benita rattled off the information, and when she hung up, Natasha reluctantly dialed Logan's number to cancel.

He'd lied. Logan revved his motorcycle past another yellow light, not feeling the least bit guilty for the whopper he'd told Tasha. Two years of synchronizing his East and West Coast businesses pretty much guaranteed he was no technological greenhorn.

He could've set his computer up, but, man, he wanted to see her again. To feel her mouth on his, her skin against his, and yes, even if it took all night, he wanted to hear her song of moans that led to her orgasms.

Of course, there had been a connectivity error! It would've been a miracle if they'd connected at all.

Maybe in the future, he assured himself, the online fantasy would be possible, but just not now.

Why? He turned the question around in his mind, trying to find an answer that didn't sound like he was becoming seriously pussy-whipped.

He pulled up to a red light, waiting to turn left, when the wireless connection on his helmet double-beeped, indicating a recent voice mail. Since he was waiting for the light to change, he pressed a switch in his customized dashboard and the message began to play.

"Logan? Dammit, I was really hoping to catch you. . . . Sorry for the short notice, but something important has come up and I need to cancel with you tonight. I, ah, hate to do this but, I'll call you later, okay? Unless it's just too late then I'll call you tomorrow." There was a short, uncomfortable pause. "Okay, good night."

The car behind Logan honked, and he realized the light had changed to green. He made an illegal U-turn and started back.

What could possibly be more important than a good night of sex? Family was the only answer. It got him thinking about seeing Benita at the hospital. Hell, if that was the case, the night was truly over.

The excitement that had been bubbling inside him began to slowly fizzle. He took the freeway ramp and focused on the speed of the wind, suddenly needing the cold night to clear his mind.

Thirteen

The restaurant was impeccable, the art deco interior was exquisite, and the tension that spanned the table between Natasha and her mother was almost toxic.

"I hear it's going to rain tomorrow," Benita said, not even looking up from the menu she was perusing.

Natasha peered over her own menu. Small talk? From her mother? "I haven't checked the weather report yet."

Another short pause followed as they both studied their menus before the waiter arrived to take their order.

Once he was gone, Natasha took a sip of her water glass. "So, what's the bad news?"

Benita carefully straightened the napkin on her lap. "Before we get into that, I want to talk about Mr. Taylor."

"Well, I don't." Natasha took her own napkin off her lap. "I don't have time for this, Mom. I thought you had something more important to discuss than that. I don't want to start a fight, Mom, but—"

"Wait." Benita's face looked pinched. "Let me just have my say."

Natasha sat back, fuming. Waiting.

"You're a big girl, I know. I worry about you, that's all. He's the kind of man who could hurt you, and I don't mean physically."

"No more than Eugene did," Natasha countered.

Benita's frown deepened. "Everyone thought Eugene was a fine man."

"And look how he turned out."

"Natasha, I'm not arguing with you. I'm only saying that Logan Taylor just might be worse than Eugene."

"I think that's for me to decide, don't you?"

With the tact of a pro, the waiter approached the table, served appetizers, and disappeared.

Natasha took a stuffed mushroom and placed it on her serving plate but couldn't work up the appetite to eat it.

"I'm sorry," Benita finally spoke, reaching for her own stuffed mushroom. "I just felt the need to warn you about him."

Natasha cut the mushroom in half just to have something to do, then took a bite. *I canceled with Logan for this?*

Benita sighed, watching her fork as if she was speaking to it. "I have a cyst in my ovary. Early stages of cancer. My doctor assures me we were lucky to catch it so early."

The mushroom lodged somewhere in Natasha's throat before she forced it down. "What?"

Rather than repeating what she'd said, Benita simply nodded. "It probably sounds worse than it is. No big deal. Your father made me promise I'd tell you."

Just like that? I have cancer, pass the salt?

The pressure that had formed in Natasha's throat seemed to have moved down to her chest. It was *cancer*, for chrissakes! Of course it was a big deal! Especially if Benita was trying to make light of it.

Okay, so they may have caught it in the early stages, but was that an ironclad guarantee that the condition was only temporary? What if it wasn't temporary? And how in the name of God could this have happened to the powerful, indomitable Benita Madison?

Not knowing what else to say, Natasha exhaled the breath she'd been holding. "I'm so sorry, Mom."

Benita shrugged, as if adjusting a heavy purse strap. "Apparently life happens, although it's taken me a while to get the memo. But," Benita flashed a jury-winning smile, "it certainly makes a person reevaluate her life. It's the only reason I'm sticking my nose in your business. I don't want you to make any mistakes you will live to regret. I know I, ah, haven't exactly been spouting advice in the past, but believe it or not, I see how much potential you have, how smart you are, and all the goodness you have to offer the world. Or even a man."

"Mom—"

"I know, I know. I said I wouldn't talk about it."

As if sensing the volatile mood at the table, the approaching waiter made quick work of placing their main courses on the table before hurrying off.

The grilled salmon Natasha had ordered sat in a perfect bed of brown rice, a whiskey-dark glaze topping the grill marks. Artfully placed green and red spots of sauce decorated it. Her mother's dish was an elaborate, colorful salad with rings of calamari peppered on top.

Neither of them made a move to eat.

"When did you find out?" Natasha asked.

"A couple of weeks ago."

Had her mother intended to tell her during the infamous birthday lunch?

"What's the next step?" Natasha asked. "When do you start treatment?"

"In a couple of days." The apprehension etched on Benita's face could not be disguised, and Natasha had a sudden urge to reach for her mother's hand, to comfort her in some way.

She leaned forward, braving the contact and discovering her mother's fingers were cold to the touch. "Is there anything I can do to help?"

Benita's smile looked tortured. "I don't think so."

Natasha wished her father was with them. He always knew the right thing to say.

With an overly bright smile and watery eyes, Benita shifted her hand out of reach and waved it in the air as if an invisible magic wand would handle all the problems. "I was hoping to break the news to you with a little less drama, dear."

Benita picked up her fork, determinedly attacking her food. "My salad looks good and I don't want to spoil it with talk about chemotherapy or other medical treatments."

Christ. Natasha casually placed her hand back on her lap.

"In fact," Benita continued, "I'd rather get your opinion on the Ramsey case."

For a moment, Natasha almost changed the subject back to

Benita's cancer, but her mother was looking at her with such a stubborn plea that Natasha conceded and began to talk about the Ramsey file.

She'd have to find a way to discuss the cancer in more detail with her mother, but apparently, it wasn't going to be tonight.

After the long ride on his motorcycle, Logan ended up parking in front of the bistro where he'd met Natasha. Back when she wanted to pretend there was no chemistry between them.

By the look of things, a late-night poetry jam session had just ended, and the crowd of fans, mostly wearing black, was already dispersing.

Logan ordered a decaf and settled into the window seat, just as he had the last time. He could've been anywhere else, he reasoned. Could've jumped in the boxing ring for a few workout rounds with Ivan. Could've gone to the rock-reggae party that was no doubt shaking the walls at his club.

He could've been anywhere else but in the bistro, doing a shit-poor job of avoiding the reasons he was there to begin with.

He blew at the hot froth topping his coffee before taking a drink. He missed her. *Missed* was probably the wrong word. Obsessed? It was beginning to feel more like it. She was a mystery to be unraveled. A problem to be tangled or untangled in different ways every time they met. Yes, she was addictive.

Reaching into his jacket, he extracted his PDA, then scrolled through his e-mails. There was one from the Orchid Soul maintenance staff, stating that "recent problems with the system are being addressed," making it necessary to take the system down on the weekend. It was followed by a side note that Eileen was doing better and improving daily.

Logan had visited Eileen in the hospital when she'd looked pretty raw. He was glad to hear the good news. Nonetheless, there was now a new countdown for Orchid Soul. What did that mean for him and Natasha?

He finished his coffee and was about to head out when he looked out the window and saw her stop at the sidewalk, looking in. Her gaze fixed on his, surprise clear on her face. He hadn't expected his heart to give a kick like it did, filling with uncontrolled joy.

He watched her approach the bistro, heading directly for the counter. So he settled back into his chair, feeling apprehensive.

Even before she joined him at his table, he could tell something was up. "Hi."

"Hi."

"I got your message. Is everything okay?"

Even her smile was weak. "A family thing came up."

"Oh."

She absently touched her hoop earring. "I got your evaluation e-mail."

"What e-mail?"

She paused. "Swear to God, Logan, it's been a long night. Don't bother playing games."

Her stubborn look had him frowning. "No games. I haven't filled out any evaluations."

She contemplated her coffee. Then, looking annoyed, she reached into her purse, flipped open her PDA, clicked a few things, and handed it to him.

He read:

> Your fantasy date has decided to no longer pursue further fan-
> tasy dates and has indicated "low-rated feedback" as the evalu-
> ating reason. He has requested to conclude the relationship with
> you at the receipt of this notice. Be assured that this is not a re-
> flection of your attraction, your communication, or your mutual
> desires. It merely means that he is no longer an interested party
> and would like to thank you for your time and participation, while
> wishing you the best of luck in all your future endeavors.

The remaining sentences were not-so-subtle legal reminders to cease and desist, basically designed to discourage any stalker-like behavior.

It was a hell of Dear John letter.

Especially since he had nothing to do with it.

He handed her the PDA back. "Did you, even for moment, seriously think I would send you that?"

Her eyes flashed amusement. "I had my doubts, but truthfully, I never know what to expect."

"Well, for one, I don't let dating services do my breakups for me. It must be another bug."

"Aha." Her lips actually formed a small smile.

Who put that sad look in your eyes? Talk to me, babe. The endearment popped into his head unheeded, flustering him a bit. She warmed her hands on her coffee mug, and as he watched her, he tried to identify the feeling going through him.

Natasha tucked a strand of hair away. "Sorry, not up for much conversation tonight."

He dared to ask, "What's wrong?"

"It's . . . personal."

Part of him wanted to stay out of it—he couldn't help but feel the sting of her words.

"Anything I can help you with?" he finally asked.

"No."

She set aside the coffee even though it was still pretty full. "I should go. Lots of job hunting to do tomorrow."

"Need a ride home?"

"I'll walk. It's not far."

"I know."

"Oh, yes. I'd forgotten."

"I have a spare helmet—"

"No!" She looked like she was repressing a sigh. "Sorry. I mean, no, thanks."

Okay. So, she wanted to be alone. "Alrighty." He finished the dregs of what remained in his mug, then reached for his helmet.

She also stood.

They both walked outside, and with a wave of her fingers, she started to walk away, her arms crossed, her clutch purse tight under her arm, as if bracing for a storm.

He straddled his motorcycle, watching her. On a night like this, he was going to have to trail her home, that was all there was to it.

He was about to slip the helmet on when he saw her stop and glance over her shoulder at him. He lowered the helmet, waiting. She stood like a statue, still looking at him for a good ten seconds.

Then, to his surprise, she walked back toward him, stopping next to his motorcycle.

"Can I ask you a favor?" she asked, the words sounding stiff from her lips.

"Sure." Anything.

She closed her sad eyes momentarily, and when they opened, their depths looked dark and wounded. "Can you come home with me tonight? I just . . . I don't want any questions."

No questions. No answers. But she needed him enough to ask.

As a reply, he handed her his helmet and retrieved the second helmet for himself.

"Thanks," she said, the helmet muffling her words. Her arms went around him when he started the bike.

"Hold tight," he said, but he drove carefully from the parking lot, aware of every inch of her against him.

Natasha closed her eyes most of the way home. Once they arrived, no words were spoken as she unlocked the door to her house and they stepped into the dark foyer.

She locked the door, and even with her back to him, she was aware of his setting the helmets down and waiting.

At the very least, she owed him some sort of explanation, right? But why burden him with what was on her mind? Why force him to go through the motions of caring? Wasn't it easier to give them both what they wanted?

"Tasha?"

Ah, that lovely nickname. She stepped up to him and brushed her lips against his, sinking into the strength of his arms, everything else fading under the tender patience of his kiss.

Passion pooled like a slow heat, licked from tongue to tongue, from breath to gasp, growing like his erection against her hips, sharpening to an edge of desperation.

She tore at his shirt.

He fumbled with the buttons of her dress.

On her shoves, they stumbled their way to the bedroom, leaving clothes in their wake.

Goddamn his mouth! Goddamn him, she couldn't get enough! His hand slid down over her belly, his fingers zeroing south, seeking her clit and rubbing over it as he slid two fingers into her wet pussy.

She rocked against him, moaning, and wanting only sweet, selfish release.

"Babe . . . Tasha, hold on . . ."

She tuned his words out, listening only to the tone of his need, his hard breathing and the incredible certainty of his touch.

She trembled when his mouth found the pulse under her jaw, felt the world tip when they fell into bed, and damn near fell apart when he guided his cock into her, thick and hot and so deep that she tossed her head at the pleasure.

"Babe . . ."

He was moving inside her, deeper, his mouth over hers, whispering things that sounded like promises but wrapped in profanity. His hand cupped her achy breast, molding the sensitive weight before he slanted a kiss over it, as if it were her mouth. She clutched him, the pleasure curling her toes so that she locked her legs over his buttocks.

"Logan . . ." She arched, beginning to inhale, her breath stuttering on her lips as the orgasm struck, trapping the air in her lungs, uncurling in her womb like a splash, twitching and gripping there, slippery and rough and hard. She squirmed against him, wringing out every last wave of pleasure until she was swamped in the shaky aftermath.

He was everywhere. On her. In her. Around her.

The echo of his heartfelt groan rang in her ear, the warmth of it caressing her neck.

Little by little, the muscles in her legs felt like they were turning into butter. Her legs slid to the back of his thighs and she realized he still had his jeans around his knees.

They lay unmoving for a long while, but unlike the past, Natasha didn't feel sleepy in the least. She looked up and noticed Logan watching her, sweat gleaming on his forehead, his braids framing his handsome face.

He touched her face, his fingers caressing her cheek, then moving to her ear to trace the sensitive outline. Not once did his eyes stray from hers.

It had been selfish to want him, to ask him to come over. And it was such a sweet delicious thrill to know that he'd come anyway. Damned if she hadn't just complicated things further.

Messy. Wasn't that the term he'd used a while back?

"We should clean up," she murmured.

He dropped a kiss on the tip of her nose, then rolled off her. Moments later, he'd removed the condom, along with the last of his clothes.

Without a glance at her, he went into her bathroom and started the shower.

Hell, she should've at least thanked him. She covered her face with her hands, squelching the urge to give a short, brief growl of self-disgust.

God, what had she done?

He was an excellent lover, but their friendship was fragile. Dammit, where did that leave her?

Logan Pussy-whipped Taylor.

It had a ring to it, he mocked himself. His brother had been right.

Despite the troubled look in Natasha's eyes, Logan wanted her. He also wanted to ease whatever was bothering her. She'd looked so vulnerable when she'd asked him to come home with her.

No, he wasn't pussy-whipped. That implied he'd been thinking with his cock, and frankly, he hadn't been thinking with his cock or his brain.

Which left only his heart. And that was the scary god-damned truth.

Shit.

She'd said she wanted to shower alone, so he'd let her, even though it made him feel hollow. Now, here he was, lying in the dark next to her, feeling overly protective, and sensing she was close to tears.

Screw it!

He turned toward her, moving in until his naked front spooned up to her naked back. She immediately stiffened, but he didn't care. Pulling the blankets over them, he anchored one arm around her waist, his hand landing just under her breast, and slid the other arm under her pillow.

"Logan, I don't need—"

"Shh."

About five minutes drifted by before she moved her hand to cover the one he held at her waist. Under his hand, her breathing grew short and choppy, and when he leaned over, her silent tears were sliding into the pillow.

A brutal, utter helplessness tore into him.

Unable to stand it any longer, he said, "Tasha, talk to me, babe."

She squeezed her eyes shut and shook her head.

He fought several instincts as he slowly eased back down. When he tried to move his hand away, she clamped down on it.

He heard her swallow past whatever emotion was at her throat, then she reached for the box of tissues by the bed and plucked several of them.

"Christ, you're crying."

"No, I'm not.

One minute she was looking at him over her shoulder with bleary eyes and the next, his arms were filled with her, her embrace tight and hard, her body straining with what it took her to keep from crying.

At a loss for what to do next, he simply held her. As the seconds drew out, her pose gradually softened, and her tears burned his shoulder as he fumbled to find words of comfort, wishing he knew exactly what to say.

At one point, he reached over her to the bedside table, grabbed several tissues, and pressed them into her hand, kissing her forehead.

She mumbled her thanks and blew her nose, her tears dampening his chest where her face touched him. He caressed hair from her face, still murmuring to her, feeling the emotion she was still trying to hold back from him.

"Can I have more tissue, please?"

He half covered her with his body to reach for the tissue box, grabbed several more, and handed them to her.

After a long stretch of time in which he rubbed her back and listened to her sniffles fade, he tipped her face to his. "You okay?"

She nodded, her eyes still glistening with tears she seemed determined not to spill. Unexpectedly she touched her lips to his for several seconds, then hid her face back against his chest.

About twenty more minutes drifted by before she spoke again. This time her voice was solemn. "My mother says she's been diagnosed with cancer."

Damn. "Tasha, I'm sorry."

Her hand fisted against his chest.

"What kind?"

"Ovarian." She paused, swallowed audibly. "But she says it's in the early stages."

"Medicine has come a long way. Her odds are good at the early stages."

Her eyes met his briefly. "I think she kept it a secret for a while. My father made her tell me. Can you believe that? Why wouldn't she tell me on her own?"

He didn't know what to say, so he didn't say anything.

"I mean, would I ever have known? Don't I have the right to know?"

The little voice telling him to shut up went unheard. "Well, I didn't want to mention it, in case it was nothing, but I saw Benita at the hospital parking lot when I was dropping Ivan off."

Natasha blinked and frowned at him as if she hadn't understood a word he'd said. "What?"

Since she was looking him dead in the eye, he continued. "I noticed her in the parking lot. She seemed a bit upset, but I had no way of knowing what it was about."

"Upset? Was she crying?"

Crap. "I guess? I don't know—"

"And you didn't tell me?"

"What was there to tell?"

She shifted to move away from him.

"Dammit, Tasha," he said, holding her. "I saw her at the hospital, but that didn't make me think she has cancer. For all I knew, she was visiting a friend who was in a bad way. What would be the point in telling you any of it?"

Her eyes flashed with anger and tears. "It seems that everyone has a secret."

"If I'd told you, do you think it would've changed anything?"

She glared at him, but her resentment gradually faded. "No, I guess not." She lay back down with him. "I guess I wish she would've told me herself."

Even though the conversation died, he held her for hours before she finally slept. Only then did he sleep as well.

Natasha awoke from a dark, motionless sleep, peering through her lids at the soft, golden light that announced the early morning dawn. She felt the touch of something delicate and soft on her forehead—for just a second, then it was gone.

She waved at it with her hand, but this time, an audible, light pop had her half sitting on the bed, clutching the bedsheets to her chest, to find that she was surrounded by falling . . .

"Bubbles?" She puzzled at the sight, then blinked again to be sure she wasn't dreaming. She spotted Logan beside the bed, naked except for his jeans, blowing more bubbles over her.

"What are you doing?," she asked, suddenly feeling like a kid seeing snow for the first time.

"Waking you up." He grinned and sent another stream of bubbles cascading over her.

She chuckled and fell back to the bed, waving her hands to touch as many of the fragile, gleaming orbs as possible.

It felt unreal and somewhat magical. She grinned as the bubbles burst on her skin like little kisses, the soft light that flirted over them showing off their iridescent colors.

When the last of the bubbles spiraled down, she crossed her arms over her naked breasts, still beaming up at him. She was dying to ask "Why?" but decided on, "That was nice, thank you."

He shrugged, screwed the lid back on the small bubble bottle he held, and placed it on the bedside table.

"You slept through the first twenty minutes," he said as he reached for his shirt, his grin warming to a smile.

She ran a hand over her hair, her curls feeling like intertwined vines with a life of their own.

He'd moved on to his boots, lacing them without looking down, his gaze trailing over her face. "I got a call from work, so I have to head out."

"I can whip up some breakfast," she volunteered, already scooting to the edge of the bed.

"No, thanks." He searched her wooden floor until he spotted his wallet in a corner. It must've fallen out of his pocket on their race to the bed the night before.

He dug his keys from his front pocket, then leaned over her, his coffee-scented kiss making her want to pull him into the bed.

"You've had coffee!" she said, realizing he'd been up longer than she'd suspected.

"I left half a pot for you. Hope you like it strong."

Like my man? "Yes."

"I really hate to go, especially after last night, but something's come up. I'll catch up with you later, okay?"

"Um, sure."

"Okay." Seconds later, he was gone, slipping his bulky jacket on as he headed for her front door, leaving behind the scent of sex and bubbles.

Fourteen ❧

That morning, Natasha called her friends to inform them of her mother's cancer, commiserating with them only briefly, since they were both at work. Rusty offered her hugs and kisses, while Vanessa offered up one of her "fix you right up" bouquets. It was like balm on the soul.

Afterward, she hit the Internet in search of information on ovarian cancer and finally stopped when she realized she was panicking even more.

To regain some normalcy, she began updating her résumé, then stopped just when she was about to go online to do some job hunting. It wasn't about another nine-to-five job anymore. Why not aim higher? She could dream, couldn't she?

Heck, Logan had shown her that happiness could come at any time, in many ways. What if she tried to sell happiness? Ridiculous. But her thoughts strayed to the bubbles and from there to the pearls, and to flowers . . . until the fledgling idea began to take shape in her mind.

Hadn't she seen a "For Rent" sign in the empty corner store in the quaint neighborhood not far from her home? It was tiny but perfect for a small starter business, such as a boutique, where she could sell things that made people happy! Yes, maybe start with women's accessories, along with something just a touch quirky, like small bubble bottles—anything to make it feel like a best friend's hangout. She'd have some closet items like unique shoes or custom frills, some sinful chocolate, and maybe even some chick-flicks. In fact, a bubble machine would be just the thing to have at the door to greet the clientele every time they stepped in. She'd call it "Happiness Is."

Excited about her new plan, she began scribbling notes until she realized it was almost noon.

She made a quick sandwich and returned to her desk, deciding to take a break to check her e-mail messages. There were two from Orchid Soul and one from her father. She skipped the Orchid Soul e-mails and went directly to her father's.

> The surgery is scheduled for this Friday @ 10:00 a.m. Can you make it?

She immediately grabbed her phone and called him. "Hey, Dad."

"Pumpkin!"

"Busy?"

"I always have time for you."

It meant he was swamped. "I'll be brief. I just wanted to let you know I'll be there for Mom's surgery."

He seemed relieved. "Thanks, honey. I didn't doubt that you would be." He started to explain about the lengthy, complicated surgery, trying to reduce it to a less involved process, and she realized he was more nervous than he was letting on.

"It'll be fine, Dad. I'll be there," she promised.

They said their good-byes, and she hung up.

Then she eyed the remaining two e-mails. There was enough going on in her life without Orchid Soul. Still, curiosity got the best of her, and she opened up the first e-mail to find a message from Orchid Soul stating they would shut the system down, with a side note that Eileen was improving at the hospital.

Natasha made a note to send her friend flowers.

The second Orchid Soul e-mail was from Logan—a short and concise fantasy.

Sex on a motorcycle. Mine. Dress any way you like.

"Impossible," she murmured, but her mind had already conjured up the image. The logistics would be tricky.

Logan always looked good on his motorcycle, so why not? For a few precious seconds, she stared off into space, letting her imagination get the best of her before reality hit her.

Hell, there was no time for that. Priorities had changed practically overnight. Orchid Soul would just have to wait. And if the former e-mail was right, the wait might turn out to be indefinite.

Benita Morgan did something she never thought she'd do. She kidnapped her husband.

"I thought we were going out to lunch," he asked as they drove by their favorite restaurant.

"We are. To Salsboro's."

Peripherally, she saw him turn toward her. "In Vacaville?"

"That's the one."

"It's an hour away."

"Just about."

He paused a moment, running his hand over his seatbelt, still watching her. "Darling, what's going on?"

She kept her eyes on the road. "I've cleared your calendar for the day. For lunch."

His lack of response told her how surprised he was.

"You don't mind, do you?" She took a split second to glance away from the road. "I just wanted you all to myself this afternoon."

His hand slid to the back of her neck, massaging her nape. "Really? Who are you, and what have you done to my wife?"

She chuckled. "She's been replaced by me, Benita, version two-point-oh."

"What was wrong with version one?"

"Too many bugs," she admitted with a little trouble. "Her good-wife chip was especially iffy. Version two comes with outstanding new and improved features."

She turned to catch his grin of pure delight. "Ohh. Sounds interesting. Such as?"

She tipped her head in thought. "Kidnapping. Assault with soft, fuzzy handcuffs."

He chuckled. "Criminal features? Are you crossing over to the other side of the law?"

"Yup, and I'm taking you with me."

His thumb trailed over her hoop earring. "Okay, version two, I'll go wherever you want to take me. But for the record, I was perfectly fine with version one."

She blindly reached for his hand, then brought it to her lips to kiss. "Thank you."

"You're welcome." He reversed the hold of her hand and brought her fingers to his lips. "Darling, you're not trying to get out of the surgery, are you?"

"No. Are you kidding? It's a minor thing."

He held her hand when she would've pulled back. "You're nervous. Just like when you were pregnant with Natasha and we were rushing to the hospital because your contractions were getting stronger. Remember?"

"I remember the bastards sending me home because the contractions weren't close enough to suit them."

"But you went in, and twelve hours later, we had the world's loveliest little girl."

Even scrunched up and wailing her head off, Natasha had been a gorgeous baby. "Those twelve hours broke down into some very ugly, painful pushing sessions."

"Is that what sticks in your mind?" The quiet tone of his voice drew her attention momentarily to him. Hell, what had she said? A quick mental replay of the conversation had her revaluating her answer.

"Of course it wasn't all bad, hon. I remember you by my side the entire time, holding my hand, massaging my feet, sneaking me ice even when the nurses said I shouldn't have any. I remember how insanely happy I was to hold my daughter in my hands. My pride and joy. My very own daughter! But you looked like you'd turned into Superman with her in your arms . . . It all seems like it was just yesterday."

"It was," he agreed. "Just not in calendar days."

She briefly squeezed his fingers. "So, something tells me you're too good of an attorney to reminisce for no reason. What are you driving at?"

He squeezed back, then carefully released her hand. "You're not trying to interfere in Natasha's life, are you? I won't do it, you know? She's a big girl. She can handle her future any which way she wants."

Lately, he'd been so neutral. They'd always seen eye to eye on almost everything, so why not on this? Did he not see how important it was to her? Since when was wanting the best for their daughter a bad thing? It was uncomfortably sobering. "I worry about her, dear. Do you believe that Logan could be good for her? Seriously."

A few seconds followed before his hand covered hers. "Let's just say that he may not be bad for her."

"You can't really believe that!"

"I do. She could do worse. He's focused, smart, and seems to have integrity."

"*Seems to* isn't enough."

"He's also ambitious and profitable."

"So was Eugene."

He laughed. He actually laughed! "The only thing Eugene had was the ambition. I advised you not to meddle then, just like I'm advising you not to meddle now."

"I'm not meddling."

"Benita, you are. When are you going to admit Eugene was all wrong for her?"

She gripped the steering wheel tighter. "Okay, so if Eugene was bad for her and she had a rough recovery, how much worse do you think Logan Taylor is going to be?"

He drummed his fingers against his thigh. "Are the meddling features on Benita version two modifiable?"

She flashed him a phony smile. "You're so funny! Cute and funny."

"I take it the answer is no?"

"We're a team, right? She's got a law degree, she's beautiful, she's got potential—"

"Benita, you have surgery coming up. How about you focus on that for the next few days?"

"That *is* my focus. I'm doing this because I'm her mother and I care. Heck, I could die during surgery, you know."

He sat in absolute silence for three seconds before he unleashed a string of pent-up profanities that had her tapping her brakes in surprise and pulling over to the curb.

"Goddammit, Benita, I love you, God knows I do. But you are not allowed to pull that shit on me!" He glared out his window. "You don't get to say we're having lunch then play the death card. You don't get to butter me up to use me against our daughter. And you sure as hell don't have to kidnap me to have me. History doesn't always repeat itself, you know? I've been with you all along. I love you, dammit. I *love* you! So, no, you don't get to say that to me. Ever."

"Calm down, hon—"

"Just . . . forget lunch, I'm not hungry anymore."

"Honey, please—"

"No. Right at this moment, it's not about you, Benita. It's about our daughter, and the choices *she* has to make in her life.

She doesn't need you to *fix* anything. It's about her! And if you care to notice, occasionally, it's about me, too."

Before she could say anything more, he stepped out of the car and walked away, ignoring her calls.

Fifteen ❧

M istaken identity," Ivan muttered through clenched teeth. "I just spent the last three hours being fucking questioned because I'm an ex-con, and they didn't think they had to look any further."

"You fit the description. Tall with an eagle tattoo."

"On the shoulder, not on the arm!"

"I know."

"Fuck!" He fumed as Logan drove. "The only reason they let me go is because the motherfucker held up another gas station and got caught. Otherwise I'd be in there, listening to them goddamn yapping about me only being a 'person of interest' while they eat their fucking donuts! That shit is unbelievable!"

Ivan was blowing steam, and Logan wasn't sure he was about to stop anytime soon. It hadn't helped that Ivan had been about to go on a date and consequently had stood up his date. "It's over. Forget about them."

Ivan seemed defeated, slumping slightly in his seat. "No, I *thought* it was over, but it's not. I'll always be on their radar. I'll be the first guy they think of that fits their six-foot-Caucasian-with-a-tattoo profile."

"Welcome to my world. Well, except for the Caucasian part. I stopped counting the number of times I've had to show my license and registration for no reason at all. It's just what happens when people are threatened by you. They become suspicious of you, and you become a target. They believe what they want to believe. You've got to move on."

"Shit, when was the last time you were pulled over?"

"It's been a while." Logan grinned. "I moved on and got me some bona fide, sue-happy lawyers."

"Right, well, I'll start saving up for that." But at least Ivan looked like he'd calmed down a bit.

"Ivan, I didn't want you moving back into that old neighborhood anyway. The crime and violence is worse than it was years ago. I know you're worried about rent money, but—"

"I'm not asking you for anything, Logan."

"You don't have to. We're family."

"I'm not asking you to take care of me. Today was different, an isolated case."

"I know." They came to a red light, and Logan glanced at Ivan. "I'm just giving you a place to stay, away from people with suspicious natures. Hell, someday, who knows? My old ball and chain may boot me to the doghouse and guess who I'll be callin'?"

That brought a reluctant, weary smile to Ivan's lips. "Ball and chain, huh?"

Logan shrugged and focused on a woman pushing her stroller across the street. "You never know."

From the corner of his eye, he could see Ivan looking in the opposite direction, as if in thought. Just before the light turned green again, Ivan said, "Thanks, man."

"You bet."

On the date of her mother's surgery, Natasha got a text message from Rusty, who had to work early but wanted Natasha to know that she was going to pray for Benita. Vanessa called to say the same, asking Natasha to stop by her flower shop to pick up some pink tulips she'd made especially for Benita.

It was hard not to think about what could go wrong during surgery.

Natasha greeted her father with a hug when she spotted him in the hospital prep room.

"Hey, baby," he hugged her tighter than he usually did. "I'm so glad you came, pumpkin. She's in the bathroom, putting on that stylish hospital gown."

Natasha squeezed him back. "How're you holding up?"

"I know I have the easy part of waiting, but I still want it over with."

"And Mom?"

Benita chose that moment to step out of the small bathroom, holding the drab hospital gown closed for dear life. "I don't see why they won't just let me wear my robe. Caleb, dear, I think if you ask—Oh! Hi, Natasha."

"Hi, Mom. Brought you some flowers." There was an awkward pause before she moved from her father's side to kiss her mother's cheek.

Benita looked surprised, and for once, Natasha honestly

thought her mother was at a loss for words. Ever the gentleman, her father handed Benita a blanket, which she instantly tucked around herself while Natasha plopped the flowers by the bedside table.

"It'll be in and out, you know," Benita said, watching them with anxiety on her face.

"It's an easy procedure," Natasha assured her.

Her father nodded, looking a bit watery-eyed. Sure, he could argue hard cases before tough juries and even tougher judges, but at the moment, he looked like he was about to fall apart like a kid who just lost his puppy.

"How are you and your boyfriend doing?" Benita asked.

Natasha bit her tongue to hold back a retort, then took a calming breath and asked, "I hear the surgery should be about an hour or so?"

"It's all right to talk about Logan Taylor, dear. I assume you're still dating him, right?"

"Benita." Caleb only said her name, but it effectively ended the conversation.

"What? It's an innocent question."

Caleb shook his head.

To avoid a conflict, Natasha replied. "You're about to go into surgery, Mom. How about we talk about something else?"

Thankfully, the nurse came in to prep Benita, and from then on, time started to grind down the minutes like hard crystal.

It was hours later when the doctor assured Natasha and her father that the surgery had gone well and that Benita was in recovery. For the first time since the surgery, Caleb sat and took a deep breath. Natasha massaged his tense shoulders, not quite knowing how to comfort him.

"Thanks for coming," he said. "I'm really glad you were

here. Your mom's a strong woman, but I know she's really glad you came, too."

"Not coming here was not an option," Natasha replied. "Dad, regardless of what you or Mom may think of me—"

"No." He looked her in the eyes, his expression tight with intensity. "You know what? You have to make the decisions you can live with. We just love you so much, we practically want to live your life for you, but you're the only one who can do that. So, do what you want, baby. We'll be right here if you need us."

"Oh, Dad. Thanks." She laid her head on his shoulder, her heart twisting a little.

"Go home and get some sleep," he said.

But when Natasha got home, she found that she couldn't sleep. The nurses had assured her that Benita was in stable condition and should recover well. She was going to be fine. For now. And tomorrow, Natasha knew she'd have to do some serious hunting for a job.

But tonight, she just wanted to escape it all. To be with Logan and take whatever he could give her so as to forget her worries and get some soul relief.

Restless, she flipped her phone in her hand before making the decision to e-mail him.

Orchid Soul motorcycle fantasy plus Internet fantasy. My garage. 12:30 a.m.

When Logan drove his motorcycle up to Natasha's home, her garage door went up, and he was faced with a series of mirrors surrounding a spot on the ground that said, "Park here."

He'd just turned off the headlight and killed the engine when the garage door was lowered, and at the last final second before it closed shut, Natasha opened the door leading to the house.

"Welcome to Tasha's Pleasure Palace," she drawled with one hand on her jutted hip, one arm casually against the wall. She was wearing white, all skimpy lace and naughty transparency, barely covering the essentials.

Sexy as a wet dream.

And she flaunted it with the panache of an angel turning tricks in hell. Not to mention that her southern accent was far better than her German one. He tugged his helmet off and set it aside, knowing he was staring and glad to see that she was letting him.

"Damn, you're hot," he murmured.

"So is your engine," she said, eyeing his ride. It was one of his prized bikes that he rarely rode.

As he stepped off his motorcycle, he ran a hand over the cherry-red tank, all the exhaustion that had filled his day fading and leaving only a raw energy.

He wanted to remember Tasha in this sweet, bad-ass mode. Better yet, he couldn't wait to see her on his motorcycle, on his favorite power object that unified mechanics, architecture, and form. And as crazy as it sounded, he wanted to hold her close and ask about her mother. Or her job hunting. Or anything at all.

For a moment, the tings and pings of the cooling motorcycle parts crackled in the silence between them.

He took off his jacket and tossed it on one of the coatracks that she used to hold up a mirror.

"Nice setup. Are you going to give me proper welcome or what?" She practically ran up to him and jumped, wrapping herself around him, locking her legs around his hips.

"Hi there, sailor." She kissed him before he could reply, and their tongues tangled in the intimate gesture, but when they pulled apart, he could see the shadows in her eyes.

"Hey there, doll," he replied, unwilling to break the moment but still needing to ask, "How'd your day go?"

A fleeting frown came and went on her face, then she turned up her smile a few notches. "Fantastic."

"Liar." He kissed her briefly.

"Can we talk about it later?"

"If you like."

"I like."

He nodded. "Okay, then I'll just nibble these tidy whites right off your body."

This time, her smile was much more genuine. "And I'll let you, too." She shifted and wiggled away from him. "But first, I believe you signed up for some, ah, Internet porn show . . . seeing as we had to reschedule last time."

The fact that she suddenly looked a bit shy and almost fumbled the words warmed him. She averted her gaze, seemed to regroup, and when she glanced at him again, the playgirl gleam was back in her eyes.

She tugged at his shirt, then turned on her sassy mules and said, "The clock is ticking. Follow me."

He kept his gaze on the shake of her ass all the way down the hall and to her room.

He had an untamed look in his eyes, and the way he stood, with his braided hair brushing his shoulders, did nothing to hide the wildness that seemed to pulsate from him. How was it that he could get her so lust-crazed—and so quickly?

She returned to him and ran her hand along the hem of his shirt, just above his jeans, tugging it gently. Logan watched her with those sexy, predatory eyes.

"Why don't you get comfortable?" she asked, leading him to a chair she'd set just for him.

He looked her over with blatant male appreciation, his sly smile telling her he'd be patient for now. "Hmm, thanks." But he didn't sit down.

"Care for anything to drink?" she asked, stopping at the staged wet bar she'd set up in her bedroom.

He walked around her, making her feel as if the lacy lingerie had faded to nothing. He stopped behind her, the breath from his lips grazing her ear. "As corny as it sounds, you're looking like a nice, cool drink to me right now. A long, tall, Tasha."

"Oh, a cool drink, eh?"

"I think I'll have my bartender create one in your honor."

She raised her eyebrows. "And what would be in it?"

He turned her around. "Something intoxicating, with a little lush sweetness, like grenadine. And, of course, something a little tart—"

"Tart?"

His grin widened. "Maybe more than just a little."

She shifted in her heels, putting a smirk into her smile. "Go on."

"And no cherry."

She covered her chuckle with a cough. "It had better be one damned tasty, strong drink."

"Absolutely."

"You'll make millions."

"Probably . . . except I don't think I want the taste of you on anyone else's mouth." His hand came up to cup her face, his mouth slanting over hers, hard but with iron control, gobbling up her mouth at a steady, hungry pace. His other hand cupped her hip, pulling her against him and molding her against the unmistakable bulge of his erection.

He kissed her until she was feeling the thin tremble of it in her nerve endings, until her mind was getting hazy and her breathing was hot on her lips. But just when she thought he'd kiss her again, he paused.

"So what's for the online show?" he asked gruffly.

Show? Ah, yes. "Um, sit back, relax, and enjoy it."

He lowered his head and sucked her left nipple through the lace. The liquid pull of his mouth drew an instant quiver deep in her pussy.

She barely managed to bite back a moan. "N-no touching. You're supposed to pretend to be looking through a computer screen."

"I prefer the real thing." He flicked her nipple with his tongue, then turned to her other breast, his teeth clamping onto her lacy nipple with a soft bite that made it impossible not to sag against the furniture a little.

His head moved toward her cleavage, and he inhaled, but made no contact with her skin. "Are you sure there's no touching allowed?"

The flat of his palms caressed her hips, then smoothed over the curves of her butt, his thumbs impatiently riding under the thong line at her waist.

She licked her lips. "Yes. I mean, no touching."

On shaky legs, she pushed him into the plush chair, intent on getting the show started.

Logan lounged back, his full erection making a nice profile against the front of his loose-fitting jeans.

The sultry tones of Etta James poured softly from the speakers, crooning about just wanting to make love, as Natasha ran her hands over her body, easing them over her hips, over the garters, over the lacy thigh-high stockings and showing her flexibility as she bent all the way to her heeled shoes.

The enthralled expression on his face made her feel sexually powerful as he watched every step with a hunger that was almost palpable. The man was a walking, talking—sitting—turn-on!

She wanted to break him, to rule him and weaken him, and at the same time, to feel his strength, if only in his gaze.

Turning, she climbed on the bed, knowing he'd see the crotchless panties. Feeling smug, she fluffed up the pillows so she could lean back on them. By the time she'd settled against the pillows, his chest was rising and falling with his shallow breathing.

"Want to talk me through it?" she teased.

He nodded, his eyes locked with hers for a long moment. "Spread your legs."

She swallowed, tugged sensually at the hem of her thigh-high stockings, then spread her legs, careful to adjust the ridiculous heels against her comforter to reveal her trimmed pussy. The temptation to cover herself was strong, but she kept her hands on her inner thighs, remaining open to him.

Even though he was at the foot of the bed, he inhaled as if he could smell her. His hand went to his own thighs, rubbing once over his erection before going still.

Their gazes locked for a moment. "Lick your fingers, then touch yourself," he said.

Doing as he requested, she flicked her tongue over her fingers, then touched her sex, gliding over the sensitive labia before making shallow strokes over her sex.

Only when he licked his lips did she go deeper, arching just a little to suit them both.

She felt so attuned to him that she synchronized her touch to the tiniest, subtlest expression. When his fingers twitched against his thigh, she went deeper, sliding her fingers past the delicate folds and into her sex, stroking . . . stroking . . . stroking.

She moaned with the need to feel his thickness there instead of her fingers.

"Tasha."

She'd been concentrating so hard on the pleasure building deep inside her that for a bewildered moment, she wasn't even sure he'd said her name.

She caressed her clit, remembering all the times he'd greedily teased her with his warm, velvety tongue and seductive, succulent mouth.

His hand moved over his erection in a single caress.

She moved her free hand to her breast, taking pleasure in the ache tightening her nipples.

He shifted his hips, easing back to get more comfortable.

She licked her lips and worked her fingers deeper into her pussy. All these nights of fantasy sex had kept her vagina sensitive to the slightest touch, so she paced herself, taking her sweet time.

He groaned, low and deep, like a roused bear, then ran his hand over his erection again, and again.

For endless moments, she envied his hand and imagined herself stroking him. The telltale tightening started to tremble in her gut, so she slowed her strokes to prolong the sensation, staving off the orgasm.

"Logan."

"Wider. Don't close your thighs, babe."

Sweet God . . . She did as he asked, the tiny muscles of her sex stretching differently, the sensations of pleasure intensifying.

Her mouth felt slack, and she only realized her eyes had slid shut when she heard his abrupt movement and opened her eyes to see him pull his shirt over his head and toss it away.

The muscles rippled in his arms as he quickly unzipped his jeans, shucking them down to mid-thigh and freeing his hardened cock before he settled back into the chair.

When he adjusted his grip on his erection, Natasha watched as he masturbated for her. His firm cock like a trophy in his hand, his fingers caressed up and down, drawing her eye to the veined thickness of it.

The seconds drifted into each other as she adjusted her strokes to match his, her mouth watering to taste him, from the base of his impressive male stalk all the way to the bulbous tip.

As each stroke took them further, his abs tightened and the muscles on his thighs strained. The muscular flex of his pecs and forearms seemed like an extension of everything masculine about him.

She craved him deep inside her, deeper than where her fingers could reach. She wanted to feel his cock sheathing into her, feel the grind of his hip against her sensitive clit. She stroked her fingers where her imagination took her, settling for the memory of pleasure instead.

His voice was gruff when he said, "Come on, babe, come for me."

God, she was so close! "You first."

He looked utterly fascinated by her the way her hand moved over her pussy. "If I have to come over there, I'm gonna—"

"No." She arched against the pillows at her back while one hand played with her breast and the other still stroked her clit. She wanted to lose it, Lord knows she did, but she was going to wait, dammit, to have him inside her first. "Please let me see you come, Logan."

"Tasha . . ." The tip of his cock gleamed with pre-cum.

"Please."

His thighs tightened, his breathing grew even rougher.

Driven by the desire to torture him just a bit more, she rolled off the bed and unsteadily got on her knees before him, then dipped her fingers between the folds of her sex and used her wetness to anoint the ripe plumpness of his cock. Logan was practically arching off the chair as he choked up on his cock and groaned when her fingers painted over the tip, and just as she gently blew on it, his ejaculation erupted, the string of white sperm sputtering high into the air before landing on his belly and arm, each stroke pulling out just a bit more, dragging helpless grunts from him.

No man had ever done that for her. Was it like that every time he masturbated alone? It seemed to pull from deep inside him, radiating like a soft blow that washed over him. He was still struggling to catch his breath when he whispered, "Now you."

She shook her head.

"Tasha . . ."

"I'm fine," she lied. Somehow, there just wasn't going to be enough masturbation to ease the flush of fever or the yearning in her vagina. Not when she needed the body contact so fiercely.

"Get on the bed, and finish." He didn't make it sound like an option.

"I can't!"

He gave her a crooked grin. "I'll help. No, don't argue, babe, just do it."

She felt dizzy. The panting was probably leading to hyperventilation, but she sat back against the pillows and closed her eyes as she touched herself. The bed suddenly shifted and she felt his mouth on her hand, his tongue teasing between her fingers. The sensation of the two turned into a new erotic experience. He lapped her up like melting ice cream, his long fingers joining hers only for a second before pushing past her labia to slide into her vagina.

She stroked herself, allowing his tongue to take over whenever his teeth nipped at her fingers. The orgasm swirled just out of reach, then he hummed and sucked her clit into his mouth while stroking two fingers deep into her.

"God!" She tossed her head, blindly looking for release, her right hand gripping his head as the buildup of pleasure threatened to make her scream.

His fingers surged into her again, and the torture of his incredible kiss was just too much. It was as if he breathed the lightning orgasm into her, as if his velvet tongue was unleashing soul-shredding licks of pleasure that were so intense,

she hardly registered the rip of her high heels into the comforter.

Her heart felt like it had crawled to her throat. She was
huffing for air while his head was trapped between her thighs,
her hands fisted in his lovely braids. Little by little, her weak
legs parted, and he lay there, his head resting on her thigh as
exhaustion took over.

They lay still for a while, half dozing, drifting on the serene
aftermath. After a bit, he groaned, as if coming awake, then
flipped onto his back to kick off his boots and jeans.

"If you were online, you'd owe me a mint," she mumbled.

"If you were online, you'd be wearing out the batteries to
your favorite toy."

She smiled, still feeling lethargic. "I certainly would."

She kept her eyes closed when he went to the bathroom.
She heard the faucet turning, the running of water, then dozed
a bit more until she woke with her stomach rumbling and the
smells of a delicious meal floating into the room.

She took a few minutes to freshen herself up with a new
outfit, then followed the whistling coming from the kitchen.

Logan made quite the sight, all sexy and bare-chested as he
finished what looked like stir-fried veggies and chicken.

"Hey, sleepy," he said, when he spotted her. "I heard your
stomach rumbling, so I made a little something."

"My stomach would never do such a thing."

He looked away from the stove long enough to glance at
her. "Rumbled like an earthquake."

She chuckled and leaned on the counter. "Okay, maybe
it complained a little. So, you planning on feeding me, or
what?"

"Eat." He piled food on a plate and slid it on the counter toward her.

She reached for the plate, but he grabbed her wrist, then lifted her onto the counter, plopping a piece of broccoli into her mouth before she could protest. It had an unexpected spicy kick to it.

"I really like this . . . thing," he said, drawing apart the veil-like robe to get a better view of her.

"Oh, this old thing?" She used her southern accent again.

"Mmm. I like it," he said. "The accent, and the lingerie."

She playfully batted her eyelashes. "I do declare."

His grin flashed again. "I could get used to that southern accent, darlin'."

And I could get used to your cooking. She popped some chopped celery into his mouth. "Me, too."

"Yeah?"

"Mmm-hmm."

He paused. "How's your mom?"

Although part of her didn't want to deal with thoughts of her mother lying in the hospital like an invalid, her heart gave a dangerous little tug that he cared enough to ask.

"She'll be fine," Natasha replied.

He studied her, as if checking for the truth in her eyes. "I'm glad to hear it."

To avoid his gaze, she looked at his mouth and was instantly reminded of all the things he could do to her with it.

"So, you want to?" he asked.

"Hmm?" she murmured, seeing the humor in his eyes.

He licked his lips, his smile taking a devilish slant. "I asked if you want to eat this here or at the table?"

"Here's fine."

He got two forks, and they both began to eat from the overfilled dish, Logan occasionally feeding her a choice morsel while they made careful small talk.

So much needed to be said and yet, Natasha was not ready for discussion. It was up to her, she could see it in his eyes. But why ruin the night with questions that would become too personal? She wasn't with him so he could solve her problems or become her shoulder to cry on. She was with him for the sex. Mostly.

Hell.

When the dish was empty, she gathered it, along with her thoughts and the other dirty utensils, then piled them into the sink, turning her back to them.

Logan stepped into the garage to retrieve something from his saddlebags and, after a brief hesitation, she followed.

What started with a kiss next to the bike ended up with his straddling it while she straddled his lap.

Around them, the mirrors she'd set up earlier echoed every move they made, and when he lifted her hips and lowered her over his erection, she gasped and sank into him, feeling as if their reflections had turned into a silent audience.

They strained together, the shocks of the motorcycle barely complaining at the slow rhythm they were building. With each stroke he got slower, until he leaned her backward, her head resting on the speedometer, her back arching over the tank, her hands gripping the handlebars.

"Steady," he murmured, continuing to move between her

thighs like a well-oiled piston, his cock making her feel like a delicate engine trapped in a balancing act.

"God, Logan, I'm going to fall . . ." The quivering deep in her gut was building, and the growing sensations were making her breathless with pleasure.

"I've got you," he said, groaning when she shifted slightly, her vaginal muscles gripping tighter around him.

In the mirror, his hands moved to where her breasts completely spilled over the lacy bra, and she wished she was naked. At the delta of the crotchless panties, where his cock plundered, the satin fringe was gathering with each stroke to form its own caress over her clit.

Frustrated and aroused, she tossed her head, catching a glimpse of his muscular profile where he bent over her, sweat starting to glisten on his back.

He nuzzled her breasts, his breathing rugged and hot. He left love-bites on her nipples, and when their eyes met, she knew he was going to take his own sweet time exploring her.

And he made it such delicious torture.

"Don't move," he warned, just before kissing her senseless. It was the hardest thing to do—to feel his mouth devouring her, his cock moving infinitesimally inside her and to focus on holding still while the waves of desire began to crash into her.

She tore her mouth away from him. "Logan! God, I can't . . . I can't . . ."

"You can," he whispered against her lips. And the next thing she knew, she did, her hands releasing the handlebars to wrap around his shoulders, her legs gripping around his hips, keeping him deep inside her, immobile while she shuddered through the lash of a sinfully soft orgasm.

"Oooh . . ." The remainder of the moan spiraled through the cavernous garage.

Logan rested over Natasha's back. It had been three hours since they'd entered the garage, and he had no doubt that this motorcycle fantasy topped any of his other ones.

She'd draped her fabulous body over his bike and he'd enjoyed every minute of it, turning her around so she also straddled the bike, then taking her while she watched in the rearview mirror.

Most of her lingerie had fallen by the wayside, except for the thigh-high stockings and the skimpy bra.

He licked the spot right behind her neck, loving the curve leading to her spine. She gave a tiny shiver, which he had anticipated, so he licked the spot again.

It was, he realized, a testament to how much he'd come to know her. Not just sexually, although he felt really tuned in to what she liked. It was the personal thrill of knowing she hadn't done this with any man before, that she was still willing to share in their private fantasies.

He looked up to see her watching him in one of their reflections. Her full breasts were pushed against the polished red of the motorcycle tank, her gaze sleepy, seductive, and satiated. The way he leaned over her gave him the best vantage on the curve of her lower spine as it swelled to her luscious buttocks.

From there, his legs were tight against hers, the elegance of the lacy stockings a sharp contrast to his male legs. Her high-heeled white shoes were an extra touch he'd not soon forget.

Whatever martial arts she did sure gave her a fine-ass body. And even though they were mutually exhausted, his limp cock still dared to twitch inside her.

"Logan?"

"Hmm?"

"Are you done?"

Never. "Are you?"

"I could sleep for a few hours."

"I second that."

He untangled himself from her, grateful for the towel they'd used against the motorcycle seat. She went back into the house while he cleaned up his motorcycle and picked up their discarded clothes.

By the time he got back inside, he found her asleep in the tub, looking angelic, womanly, and very, very tired. He crouched down beside the tub and took a long look.

He wanted her. Damned if he didn't. And less of that want had to do with sex than it had to do with . . . man, what was it? A need to be near her? A need to *really* know her? Since when had he developed this need to be around her? Lord, she had him cooking, whistling, and feeling very . . . *domesticated*. And the hell of it was, he liked it. Really liked it.

He waited a heartbeat for the sensation of mild panic to wash over him, but it didn't. Usually, as the relationship aged, it started to fall apart at the seams. He got bored or found a personality flaw in his lover that he couldn't overlook. Or, more often than not, he discovered their ulterior motives, usually at his expense. But there was none of that with Tasha.

Taking a breath, he pushed further, going for the real fear

factors. What about pregnancy? They'd used condoms, but what if she were to get pregnant?

God.

His eyes slid to her belly, shocked at how the thought unleashed a fierce pride that had his hand hovering over the water, inches from her abdomen.

No, no, no! He stood and stepped back. What the hell was he doing? Pregnant? Did he really want her pregnant?

And then what? Was he going to be some baby's daddy?

The emotion unfurled further with more heat, and a vision of a smiley, doe-eyed, curly-headed girl popped into his head. A daughter!

Sweet Christ! He rubbed his face.

He'd never seriously though about becoming a father. No, he was a busy man, running businesses on both coasts, responsible to his staff and family, and that was about it. He worked hard, played hard, and why the hell was he thinking of a baby?

Hell.

A kid? His kid?

What kind of a father would he be? Ivan's dad was a great man, but Logan's real father had been a son-of-a-bitch with a hard backhand and a mean disposition. Science hadn't proven that it was genetic, but what if it was?

Natasha stirred in the tub, her sigh shifting the water into ripples, and he moved into action, grabbing her robe.

It was time to go. These thoughts were beyond being pussy-whipped. This was starting to feel a lot like a head-over-ass-over-heels kind of a crisis.

"Hey," he touched her cheek. "I have to go."

"Why?" she grumbled, her bleary eyes opening.

Because . . . Christ, I just realized I want to see you pregnant with my kid.

"It's late," he replied. "And you're asleep in the tub."

"Hmm. So?"

He wanted to kiss her. "I'm not leaving you asleep in the tub."

Her smile was lazy, but her eyes slid shut again. " 'Kay."

She looked adorable. Really and truly, like a worn-out lover enjoying a perfect reprieve. It brought out a primal possessiveness he'd never felt before. He wanted her to belong to him, pure and simple. No one else had the right to this . . . to her sultry kisses, her unhappy thoughts, or for that matter, any intimate part of her mind, body, or soul. Holy hell!

Had he lost his damned mind? Had love regressed him back to caveman status, for chrissakes?

Love? He swallowed dryly, letting the truth sink in.

It wasn't the thought of falling in love with her that scared him as much as the possibility that she might not feel the same way.

What would she say if he told her?

"Tasha?"

"Mmm?"

It took two more tries before she opened her eyes.

"No more fantasies," she pleaded sleepily. "Not tonight."

Hell, his fantasies had never dared to aim for love before. He touched her cheek, caressed the elegant curve of her throat. "Okay."

She made another humming sound.

He studied her lips. "I'm going to be out of town on business for the next two days."

"Mmm-hmm."

He leaned over and pressed his lips to hers, and the softness of her was almost enough to make him crawl into the tub with his clothes still on. Her eyes parted open in surprise.

"What was that for?" she asked groggily.

"Just checking to see if you're awake."

"I am."

"Good, 'cause I have to go."

"You have to?"

"Yes."

"Oh, right. Out of town."

"Yup."

"Maybe you'll come back to a new fantasy."

"Sure." Man, it was pretty sad when the luster of sex dimmed in comparison to just being with her.

He stood and retrieved her terrycloth robe. "Come on, before you prune up."

She fell asleep again the moment her head touched the pillow. Logan left the house, not sure he could return without letting her know how he felt.

Sixteen ✣

Natasha overslept, waking with a hard-biting morning headache and a sense that things hadn't ended quite right the night before, but she couldn't put her finger on it.

She wished the aspirin she swallowed with her coffee could block all thoughts of Logan, Orchid Soul, or any remote thoughts of sex. Man, she was acting like an addict after a binge, for chrissakes.

Things had to change.

Natasha found her father by Benita's bedside, looking like he hadn't slept a wink. In contrast, Benita look entirely too still as she slept.

"She'll probably sleep a bit longer," he said. "I know you want to visit Eileen, so go ahead."

Natasha kissed his cheek, touched the bedsheets covering her mother's legs, then quietly left to take the elevator two floors up.

The nurse pointed the way, and Natasha carefully opened the door. Eileen's smile greeted her, although it got a bit raggedy at the edges when Natasha hugged her.

Natasha patted her hand, mindful of the IV tube. "How are you doing? Making progress?"

"The casts will be on for a while, so I won't be jogging anytime soon." Eileen let out a long breath, smirked, and dabbed her eyes with the tissue that Natasha handed her. "Man, I thought I had it all planned so carefully, you know?"

"Had what planned?"

"Everything. My mountain-climbing trip, for example. It's the one and only time I couldn't get someone to go with me, and look at what happens."

"Murphy's Law. But look on the bright side: you made it. With a few scrapes, sure, but still in one piece. And your business is getting along just fine, so you don't need to worry about anything but your recovery."

"That's just it. The business is not getting along just fine," Eileen said, her eyes watering up again. "I had a million messages on my voice mail about how screwed up things are. And get this. I haven't been able to pay the programmers, so they're not taking my calls. Right now, I can't tell if they're holding Orchid Soul hostage, or if someone hacked in and has become the new ghost in the machine, but either way, I'm screwed!"

"Just calm down," Natasha said, hoping that Eileen's stress wouldn't set off any of the monitoring machines by the bed. "Things can't be as bad as they seem."

"But they are! It's like someone stole my business. I've put everything into this, and if I can fix the bugs now, I can salvage something. Otherwise, I lose all my money, my backers, my Web site, and my reputation goes up in smoke."

"That's not going to happen," Natasha said sternly. "If you want, I can look into it. It's probably a small misunderstanding."

Eileen looked utterly defeated. "Sure."

"I don't know much about computers, but I can talk to the programmers for you."

"Would you really? Thanks, that would be great. I'm trying to convince them to hang on for another thirty days and I'll give them a bonus, but I'm not sure how I'll do that. I really need to get the business started." Either the medication was making Eileen overly emotional or she truly was at wit's end, because her voice was pitching and her eyes watering again.

"Not to worry. Let me see what I can do, and I'll get back to you, okay?"

Eileen sniffled and managed to give her the contact info just as the nurse came to shuffle Natasha out of the room.

Natasha hugged her friend, reassured her that everything would work out, and took the elevator down to see if her mother was awake.

Benita was awake, staring at the chair where her husband had fallen asleep. The poor guy looked exhausted, and it tugged at her heart to see the faint, dark smudges under his eyes.

She'd put those there, and not necessarily with this surgery. They were partners in life, but damned if it didn't feel like he was always the one who managed to put an extra fifty percent more into everything he did. He rarely fought with Natasha, and—as painful as it was to admit it—most of the time, he was probably the better parent.

But she was trying, right? It was never too late to try to guide her daughter away from men who practically had "Mr. Wrong" tattooed on their forehead.

Caleb's forehead wrinkled while he slept, and she had the urge to kiss his brow and shoo away whatever was haunting his dreams.

She barely heard the well-oiled door swing open before Natasha stepped inside.

"Hi," Natasha whispered, waving tentatively. "How're you feeling?"

"I'm fine. I should be out of here tonight or tomorrow."

Natasha glanced at Caleb, who hadn't moved a muscle. "Want me to get him a blanket?"

"No. It'll just wake him up."

"Okay."

Seemingly without a thing more to say, Natasha moved to the opposite side of the bed and took the available chair. The dress Natasha wore swirled around her knees for a moment. No more business suits for her, Benita thought sadly.

"The flowers are from Vanessa and Rusty," she said, nodding at the gorgeous bouquet that adorned the counter next to Caleb.

"It's lovely," Benita replied. "Please thank them for me."

"They may drop by later. Well, I know Rusty has to pick up her daughter from daycare and Vanessa has been swamped at work, so they'll probably be in just before the nurses have to kick them out."

"No problem."

Natasha extracted a small bottle of water from her purse and took a nervous sip, making Benita realize she could use a drink herself. Her mouth felt like she'd tried to eat a cotton T-shirt.

Rather than ask Natasha to pour her some cool water from the pitcher next to the flowers, Benita asked, "I know your father thinks I'm meddling, but . . . are you still determined not to return to work?"

Natasha bought a few more seconds by taking another sip of water. "I'm not returning to the firm, Mom. I've decided to open up a boutique."

Benita could see the pure challenge in her daughter's gaze. Why mention that boutiques were a dime a dozen and that they hardly made much money? Did she know that the first year of business was going to be the toughest? And what about startup funds? The steady, stubborn look in Natasha's eyes said it all. "Sounds lovely, dear."

"I'm glad you approve," Natasha replied, still deadpan.

"And are you still seeing Mr. Taylor?"

Natasha put the lid back on her bottle. "Dad's right. You are meddling."

"I'm only concerned, Natasha."

Natasha looked like she wanted to roll her eyes. "About what?"

"About . . ." Benita sighed, hoping her husband was well and truly, deeply asleep. "Get me some water from that pitcher, would you?"

Natasha did as requested, then gave Benita the cup, carefully pointing the straw in the cup to Benita's lips. The ice-cold water tasted like heaven.

Natasha returned to her seat, patiently waiting.

"Your father is a great man," Benita said.

"I know."

"No, I don't think you know how great." She sighed. Hell, she'd never planned on telling this story. "When I was in high school, I fell in love with a guy. The sexy, proverbial bad boy that we mothers are always warning our daughters about. To be honest, I was in lust rather than love." Natasha's eyes widened, and Benita couldn't help but smirk. "What? I was a teenager once, too. It was all about hormones then, and I just didn't know the difference between the two."

Natasha wisely kept her mouth shut.

"Anyway, he turned out to be not so nice. It was the first time anyone ever raised his hand to me." Benita studied her hands, the memories cutting though time like a knife. "I ended up battered and pregnant halfway through my senior year."

Benita looked up to see the shock on her daughter's face. "It was the last beating that caused me to miscarry the baby, and shortly after, he died jumping off a bridge into the river. My reputation was smeared, and I hit a hard depression. It was Caleb who became my best friend, giving me encouragement, making me believe in myself, supporting my dream of being an attorney. I still remember how he saved up his money so he could surprise me with a pearl necklace to wear to my first interview." Benita smiled and glanced at her sleeping husband, then back at Natasha.

"Anyway, I guess what I'm saying is that I know a thing or two about finding a 'bad boy' attractive, but I just want you to be careful."

"I know." Natasha also glanced at Caleb, but there was new

admiration on her face. "I'm sorry you had a bad experience, Mom, but Logan is nothing like that."

"And you're certainly not a teenager either." Benita momentarily closed her eyes. They felt gritty, and she was suddenly tired again.

"You'd better get some rest while Dad's also sleeping," Natasha said. "I'll come by and visit you later."

To Benita's surprise, Natasha kissed her cheek. "Thanks for telling me the story, Mom."

The words stuck to the roof of her mouth, but Benita pushed them out. "You're welcome." Any doubts she'd had about sharing the past melted away. God willing, Natasha wouldn't make the same mistakes she'd made.

Seventeen ✿

Natasha dragged herself to the dojo and spent the next two hours practicing her kickboxing, while trying to clear her mind.

The punches jarred all the way up her shoulders, and her kicks were as hard as the ones that came back at her. Still, she couldn't banish the memory of her mother looking so helpless on the hospital bed. How was it that her mother, a woman who was damn near unconquerable, was lying in a hospital right now, as frail as an invalid? And just how many rough spots had her parents gone through that she knew nothing about?

She threw a right punch that was smartly deflected by her sparring partner, so she followed with a left hook. What was it about Logan that drew her so deeply? He was a friend, a lover, and an occasional pain in the ass. But somehow he fit in her world. But what if they'd never had Orchid Soul? Would they have ever hooked up?

Natasha's sparring partner whipped a round kick that sent her sprawling.

"You okay?" he asked, helping her stand.

"I'm just peachy," she said, speaking around her mouth guard, annoyed with herself for not paying attention. "I'm good. Really, I'm fine."

He looked skeptical, but said, "That's a wrap then. We'll do this some more next week."

They tapped gloves and walked away.

But like a cloud that hovered over her head, the turmoil of thoughts followed her.

When she got home, she showered, ate a light dinner, then checked her e-mail. It didn't disappoint to not get a message from Orchid Soul as much as not getting one from Logan. She sat in front of the computer, making several attempts to compose an e-mail to him, but ended up deleting whatever she wrote.

"Damn." She ran her hands over her face as her frustration mounted. Orchid Soul offered the perfect excuse to contact him, but without it, she felt too vulnerable. Did he feel the same way?

It was silly, but all she really wanted to do was curl up with him on the couch to catch the late news. No sex, just his quiet company. What would he think if she invited him over for dinner, without the blatant expectation of sex?

In the end, she ended up only sending an e-mail to Orchid Soul, asking whoever received her message to contact her. It wasn't great investigative work, but it was a start toward helping Eileen.

When she crawled into bed, she lay awake for a while, feeling lonely and yearning to fall asleep against Logan's chest.

Two days dragged by, filled with visits to Benita at home and Eileen at the hospital, doing research for her new business plan, sending e-mails to Orchid Soul . . . and still not hearing a word from Logan.

There had been something about him that night, but she'd been too exhausted to put her finger on it. It was the way he gently kissed her forehead before he left: she realized she was truly and hopelessly in love with the man.

How could it have happened? She braced her heart against it and had tried to squelch every hope that magically appeared. But it was like fighting a sandstorm.

This time, if her heart got ripped to shreds, she'd be worse off than the Eugene incident. It was crystal clear—as clear as every one of those facets of her Diamond Life—that she'd completely fallen in love.

Love.

Holy cow.

It was an ache that refused to ease. She finally had to move the decorative bowl full of pearls out of sight because it reminded her of him too much. But she still wore his spare shirt for her pajamas. Yup, love was sick like that.

Staying busy helped a bit. She made note of almost all the colorful accessories she was putting in her house and added them to her wish list for her store. The paperwork she put together for a business loan looked good. The lease for the boutique was reasonable, and her stomach was twisted with nerves at the thought of taking the next step.

Moreover, although she sensed it was coming, the very last thing she expected to see was a final e-mail from Orchid Soul, stating:

> Thank you for your invaluable participation in the Orchid Soul pilot project. We admit a number of unexpected issues arose, but your feedback on improving the system is greatly appreciated. Please complete the final questionnaire rating your experience, and be sure to include any additional comments you may have.
>
> On behalf of everyone at Orchid Soul, again, thank you. The test Web site will be deactivated in 48 hours.
>
> Sincerely,
> The Orchid Soul Staff

They made a sad–ass bunch. Natasha and her friends met up at the bistro for coffee, and no one seemed to have much to say.

"We're screwed," Vanessa grumbled.

Rusty smirked. "Were. Past tense," she clarified.

They were all slumped in their seats, blowing the steam from their coffee and looking dejected.

"I, for one, am glad the Orchid Soul project is finally over," Vanessa said firmly, but her expression belied her words. "The whole thing was becoming a headache."

"You mean heartache," Natasha corrected before she could stop herself.

When her friends looked questioningly at her, she shrugged.

"Or headache." Love actually could give you a headache. And a stomachache. And endless sleepless nights. Shit.

"It's not like we fell in love or anything, right?" Rusty asked quietly.

"Pfft!" Vanessa dismissed the notion after a full second.

"Impossible," Natasha muttered, right after. "It wasn't like we were looking for Mr. Right anyway. Not to say that he's Mr. Right. Mr. Right wouldn't be this argumentative and frustrating. And Mr. Right would have something on his mind rather than sex all the time, right? I mean, kudos, the man deserves an award in the sex department, but we went into this thing with our eyes wide open, and I can't say that I did not know what I was getting into. Let's get real. There was no Mr. Right in sight then, and there is none now. We're just bummed because we had a man doing the gigolo gig and we're going to miss it. We're grown women. All we need are new plans."

Both her friends looked at her as if she was quoting scripture.

"We could call them," Vanessa finally replied. "You know, to see if they're interested in keeping the same agreement."

"I don't know," Rusty hedged.

But it sounded perfect to Vanessa. "Seriously, what do we have to lose?"

Natasha avoided an answer by flashing a hopeful grin.

"The system had bugs anyway," Vanessa continued. "We can avoid that whole process, customize it any way we want, and still play."

But we're just fooling ourselves! What about love? Natasha wanted to ask.

Rusty shook her head wearily and continued sipping her coffee while Vanessa held her hand up for some reluctant high-fives.

Logan was pissed. Pissed and ready to chew his brother a new one for hiding his red swizzle sticks. A man had his limits, damn him.

Searching all the drawers of his desk hadn't produced a single swizzle stick. It didn't take a genius to realize that Ivan had taken advantage of the two days he'd been out of town to pull off the prank. Ivan had been the only one bold enough to dare to complain about seeing the chewed up plastic all over the place, but now his brother had gone too far.

The intercom on his desk buzzed, and Logan snatched up the phone. "What?"

"There's a lady here to see you, Scooter."

That did it! He was going to kick that boy's ass clear across the county, *then* fire him once and for all! Or vice versa. Goddammit! Swiveling in his chair, Logan toggled his computer settings to monitor the front door. Seeing Tasha standing there on his screen, wearing a very familiar raincoat, sent his thoughts reeling until his mind was temporarily a blank slate.

"Send her in."

"Yes, sir."

This time, Logan didn't fuss with the piles of paperwork on his desk. He stood up and walked around the desk to stand in front of it, his heart knocking as he braced himself for her.

Much too soon, Ivan opened the door and Natasha stepped in, looking so womanly and sexy that he wanted to gobble her up on the spot. It had just been a few days since he'd last seen her, lying there like a sleeping goddess in the tub. That moment had knocked him on his ass with the truth that could no longer be denied.

"Hi," she said.

"Hi." He wasn't sure when Ivan had left or if he'd said anything at all, for that matter. "Um, have a seat. Do you want something to drink?"

"No, thanks."

God, he was an idiot for her smile. The delicate scent of her perfume that was so uniquely hers was slowly wrecking his restraint. "What can I do for you?"

A flash of unease flittered across her features at the formality. "I guess you've already heard about Orchid Soul closing the pilot project."

"Yes."

"Anyway, I figured that if you're game, we could continue in our own way, so I brought you an invitation," she said, handing him an envelope that she pulled out of her coat pocket. He caught a glimpse of cleavage and wondered if she was wearing anything underneath the raincoat at all.

He tore his eyes away from her and opened the envelope to find an elaborately designed card. Inside was a lovely invitation to meet up at the stairwell where they'd first made love. Everything about it was the same. Time and place. What to wear. Instructions.

Goddammit. He wasn't starting over. Not like this. And there was no way he was going to do one more thing with her without her knowing how he felt.

It was time to yank the Band-Aid from his heart. Make that

duct tape. One hard, fast tug, and get it over with. Hopefully, his heart would mend. If there was enough left, that is.

"Well?" she asked.

"Thanks, but no thanks." He carefully slid it back into the envelope, his heart aching with each heartbeat.

"No?" She looked so alarmed, he almost felt sorry for her.

"Is that all you want from me, Tasha? More sex?"

She crossed her arms, answering neutrally. "It seemed like a suitable arrangement."

"Tell me the truth. Is it enough for you?"

She paused, looking vulnerable. "It's not enough for you?"

"Not anymore. Don't you want more?"

For several seconds neither spoke. "What if I want more than I think you're willing to give?" she asked quietly.

"Try me, Tasha. Name your wildest fantasy."

Natasha felt as if the room had spun completely around. Her wildest fantasy wasn't even a fantasy. It harbored too much reality. Lord knows she couldn't take it if he was playing a game at this point.

"Don't play games with me, Logan, just—"

"I don't want to play any more games either, Tasha."

The emotion she saw in his eyes mirrored her own in so many ways that she couldn't look away.

"Do you care for me, even just a little?" he asked softly.

She held her breath, praying with her heart. "Of course, I do."

He cupped her face. "Of course? Darling, you're killing me."

"Logan, please, just tell me what exactly you want from me."

"Everything."

She blinked and tried to wrap her mind around the single word as it speared her soul.

"Tasha, one, two, or even ten more fantasies won't do anymore. I want more. A million fantasies. One for each night for as long as I live. I want fantasies that have nothing to do with sex. I want a future. I want promises too."

"Logan . . ."

"I want to see you sleeping in my tub," he continued. "In my house. Our house."

"Our house?" It was a hoarse whisper.

"Pregnant with our child."

"Oh!" She couldn't help the choked, desperate sound that escaped her, filled with such fragile hope.

"Tasha, in my wildest fantasy, I tell you I'm crazy in love with you and there would be nothing better than spending the rest of my life with you."

"Oh my God." She grabbed his head, blinked back tears of joy and looked him in the eyes.

"I'm saying I love you, Tasha," he said, his arms wrapping around her. "Jesus Christ," he whispered. "Put me out of my misery."

She burst out, simultaneously crying and laughing, so incredibly happy she could scream. "Oh, Logan, I love you so much I can hardly think strai—"

He kissed her, pulling her into his body, filling that void that had been growing since their last night together. She sank her hands into his hair and kissed him back until they were both gasping for breath.

Logan kissed her face, repeating the words that echoed in her head. "I love you, love you, love you . . ."

For a long moment, they held on to each other, reveling in the embrace, absorbing it like sunshine.

"You know," he said, kissing her cheek, "if we have a daughter, her middle name will have to be Orchid."

"Absolutely not! That means that if we have a son his middle name would be Soul?"

"Now we're talking. Is it any wonder I love you? Let's hope for twins."

"You're nuts!"

"Triplets, then."

She chuckled as he gave her a half spin.

This truly is happiness, she thought, kissing him again.

Heck, it was pure heaven!